The TOMB BUILDER

E. JAMES HARRISON

Dear Elder & Sister Wecker — March 2017

What a great help you've been to my mom! Thanks so much for your kindness, love and concern. You've enriched her life and been a blessing.

All the best to you.

A NOVEL

The TOMB BUILDER

E. JAMES HARRISON

BONNEVILLE BOOKS
SPRINGVILLE, UTAH

ISBN 13: 978-1-59955-797-7

Published by Bonneville Books, an imprint of Cedar Fort, Inc.,
2373 W. 700 S., Springville, UT 84663
Distributed by Cedar Fort, Inc.
www.cedarfort.com

LIBRARY OF CONGRESS CATALOGING-IN-PUBLICATION DATA

Harrison, E. James, 1953- author.
 The tomb builder / E. James Harrison.
   p. cm.
 Summary: The story of the friendship between Joseph of Arimathea and Jesus Christ
   up to Christ's crucifixion and aftermath.
 ISBN 978-1-59955-797-7
 1. Jesus Christ--Fiction. 2. Joseph, of Arimathea, Saint--Fiction. I. Title.
 PS3608.A78343T66 2011
 813'.6--dc22
                              2011000410

Cover design by Angela D. Olsen
Cover design © 2011 by Lyle Mortimer
Edited and typeset by Melissa J. Caldwell

Printed in the United States of America

10 9 8 7 6 5 4 3 2 1

Printed on acid-free paper

For my family—true believers

Author's Note

Joseph of Arimathea is an enigma. Our only glimpse of him is during the final hours of Christ's life when he courageously comes on the scene, fills a supremely important role, and then slips quietly away, never to be heard of again. No one performed a more selfless act of compassion for the Savior of the world.

Joseph's role in the life of Christ was so significant that each of the Gospel writers (Matthew, Mark, Luke, and John) mentions him by name, yet we know virtually nothing about him. Biblical scholars have debated for centuries where he came from, for there is no record of a city, town, or village—either anciently or in the present—that has ever been known as Arimathea. In fact, the only reference to "Arimathea" in the entire Bible is in connection with Joseph's name.

Piecing together the few sparse details from the Gospels, we know these facts: Joseph was from Arimathea (wherever that was); he was a member of the Jewish ruling organization known as the Sanhedrin; he was immensely courageous and had exceptional moral character; he was a disciple of Christ; and he was very wealthy. We can assume a few other facts based on knowledge from other sources. For instance, Joseph was undoubtedly married and had children because the rules of the Sanhedrin wouldn't allow an unmarried and childless man to be a member. But those few facts, as tantalizing as they are, do virtually nothing to answer the question of why he did what he did. If anything, they confuse the issue. Perhaps that is why so many legends have grown up around this man—we demand answers, and when none are apparent, we invent our own.

This book adds to the legends. It is a work of fiction. Although laced together with facts and details recorded in the Old and New Testaments as well as ancient historical records, it springs from the imagination (some might say the *overactive* imagination) of the author. As for the characters, secular history—sources independent of the Bible—attests that some of the characters were real and lived during Christ's time—Caiaphas, Pilate, and Herod, for example. Others, such as Joseph's wife, were created by the author. Likewise, descriptions of geography and details about Jerusalem are a combination of fact and fiction.

One final word before plunging forward: Although this is fiction, the Man from Galilee, Jesus Christ, was not. He lived; he died; and he most definitely lives today, leaving behind an empty tomb!

—*E. James Harrison*

ONE

The night air hung heavy with dew as he cautiously walked up the street, moving silently from the shadow of one massive home to the next. The brown dust kicked up by his sandaled feet clung to the hem of his robes. He didn't mind the dust—it was all he'd ever known—but he'd already stepped in two piles of fresh oxen dung. The slippery green semi-liquid oozed between the bottom of his foot and the leather of his sandal, making walking difficult. Scurrying along in the darkness, he knew the odds of avoiding a third pile were not in his favor.

It wasn't fear for his physical safety that made him slink from shadow to shadow like a common thief, for he was a large man, a man whose very presence commanded respect. Standing over six feet tall, he towered above most people of the day, and his muscular though aging body was imposing enough to dissuade most people from arguing with him. No, it wasn't his physical safety that concerned him—it was his position and reputation. Respected members of the Sanhedrin, and wealthy ones at that, didn't roam the streets of Jerusalem at two in the morning.

He'd managed his way through the squalor of the lower city virtually unnoticed, mostly because the pathetically poor masses who occupied its one- and two-story houses, strung together like bricks in an uneven wall, had bolted the doors and shuttered the windows against thieves or worse. The lower city was a place where rats, both human and animal, roamed at will during the hours of the night.

But now he'd reached the upper city with its palatial homes. These estates, surrounded by high walls, shielded out not only intruders but also the ugliness of the lower city. Inside the walls, slaves and servants skillfully manicured the rosebushes and miniature date palms and fig trees that surrounded spacious courtyards. These rambling multi-storied homes with pillars and opulent furnishings were the residences of the wealthy merchants, Jewish high priests, and the Jewish aristocracy. It was his neighborhood.

The almost imperceptible creak of a gate hinge stopped him midstride. His instinct to flee was squelched by a desire to hide, so he slammed his back against the stone wall to make himself less visible. It was futile, of course, because the soft white light streaming from the almost full moon bathed everything in its brightness. Anyone had but to look in his direction to see him instantly. "Why did you wear a white robe?" he chided himself. "Why not black? You knew you would be out like this tonight."

The coolness of the stone wall seeped through his outer robe and linen undergarment, causing an involuntary shiver. In spite of the chill of the early April air, tiny streamlets of perspiration coursed down his back. He could feel them trickle between his shoulder blades and then race down his backbone to the small of his back, where they abruptly halted, stopped by the leather belt that held his robe in place. It wasn't exertion that caused him to sweat. It was nerves, and they were drawn as tight as a lute's strings. "Relax," he told himself, "another two hundred yards and you'll be home."

Eyes and ears straining, he looked intently in the direction from which the sound had come and silently cursed the advancing years that dimmed his night vision. Nothing! He could see no one, yet he was certain a gate had opened. If someone saw and recognized him, he would face embarrassing questions about his nocturnal travels.

"This is ridiculous," he told himself. "You're a respected member of the Sanhedrin—just walk down the street. If someone stops you, tell them you've been out discussing this Jesus of Nazareth with the other elders."

It wouldn't be a complete lie. He really had been discussing Jesus of Nazareth, but he hadn't been with the elders—he had been with the Nazarene himself. And not only Jesus, but also eight of his twelve apostles, as well as Mary, Martha, Lazarus, and perhaps twenty others. For the past several hours, they had gathered in a room in the lower city. They had all listened intently and, when invited, had even asked questions.

"Tell us, Teacher, when will the end come?" Peter had asked.

James had followed that question with one of his own: "What signs of the end should we watch for?"

"What must I do to gain eternal life?" asked an unknown man from across the room.

Joseph had sat quietly in the back of the room the entire time, churning over in his mind each question and pondering the answers. It was new doctrine—new and strange—but it was more than the doctrine. It was the man himself that had kept him spellbound.

Joseph of Arimathea was a man at odds with himself, a man whose entire world was slowly but definitely being tipped on its edge. He had spent a lifetime pursuing only two things: God and wealth—in that order. Now both were being called into question by what this man from Nazareth was teaching.

Another creak of the hinges jolted Joseph back to reality. From his position only twenty-five feet away, he could see the silhouette of a man on the opposite side of the street struggling to open the massive iron gate in the wall surrounding the palatial mansion. Having been in and out the gate many times himself, Joseph knew how much effort it took to make it swing on its hinges. This man was smaller and frailer than he, which explained the difficulty he was having.

Two thoughts raced through Joseph's mind. First, whoever the man was, he wasn't Caiaphas, the owner of the estate. Second, if the man left the courtyard and turned to his right, Joseph would certainly be seen. If he turned left, there was a chance, albeit small, that Joseph might go undetected. Joseph silently prayed the man would go left. If detected, his presence would certainly be reported to Caiaphas, the devious chief high priest, who wouldn't let it rest until he knew why Joseph was plodding about the city so late at night. Joseph's wife was Caiaphas's cousin, and being quite protective, he would assume the worst about Joseph's activity.

Of course, Joseph was equally curious what the treacherous old man was doing meeting with people at this hour. Although publicly respectful of Caiaphas, Joseph didn't hold the grizzled old man in the same regard as his wife and the masses of Jerusalem; Joseph had seen too much conniving and scheming from the man and held him in contempt.

Another creak of the gate drilled through the night air and was immediately followed by a hushed voice whispering, "Simeon, come back. Caiaphas wishes to discuss one more matter."

"Can't it wait for another day? It's far too late, and I'm beyond weary," Simeon responded loudly, not caring who might hear him.

"You must come back now. It can't wait. We still have much to do," came the hissed response.

With a disgruntled sigh, the man resigned himself to yet another long and probably sleepless night and let the gate slip from his grasp as he slowly turned back toward the house. Joseph stood motionless, listening to the fading clicks of the man's sandals as he walked across the tile flooring of the courtyard to enter the house.

Reaching to his thighs, Joseph grabbed a fistful of robe in each hand, and hiking it almost to his knees, he raced up the street in the closest thing to a run his aging body would allow. Two minutes later and completely out of breath, he pushed open the gate of his own massive estate and walked silently across the courtyard into safety and security.

TWO

"Y" ou were out late again last night," Devorah said, pouring
water from the small pot into the clay basin that stood on
a table beside him. "Where were you?"

"Talking," Joseph said nonchalantly.

"To whom and about what?" she said, her voice conveying
the slight irritation and suspicion she felt in her heart.

"To friends about God," he replied, his voice completely
devoid of emotion. Joseph would never lie to his wife, but he
didn't want to say more than was necessary. Devorah liked the
place in Jerusalem's upper society that his position and wealth
assured, and she wouldn't approve of his meeting with this
man from Galilee.

Devorah turned to face Joseph. She was slim and ener-
getic and was dressed in a flowing pink robe of a quality and
style that bespoke money—lots of it. Nature had been kind
to her. Her skin showed very few wrinkles, and her dark,
almost black hair, which she usually wore hanging loosely
to her shoulders, was highlighted with only a few streaks of
gray. This morning, though, Joseph noticed she had pulled it
back from her face and pinned it behind her ears with golden
pins studded with brilliant red rubies. Joseph admired her
beauty and marveled at how fit she was in spite of bearing

four children and forty years of marriage.

"Which friends?" she blurted, jarring Joseph back to the subject at hand.

Joseph debated his response. Telling her the truth would likely bring a repeat of the heated argument they had had several weeks before, after he told Devorah of his first meeting with Jesus. But he was tired; he had only slept for three hours since coming home and though he tried mightily, his mind simply couldn't fashion a disarming response. He turned his head toward an open window just beyond where she stood and simply said, "Jesus of Nazareth."

Joseph heard the slight sigh that escaped her at the mention of the name and anticipated what would come next.

"Not again, Joseph," she said, the distress in her voice coming through more forcefully than she wanted. "That man is nothing but trouble. He's trouble for you, for me, for my cousin Caiaphas, and for the entire Jewish people. You should know that better than anyone. Everywhere I go people talk of him. Some people are even calling him Messiah."

Joseph looked at her but said nothing. He was more than tired—he was weary. Not just physically, but mentally, and he was emotionally drained as well. After he crept home, he had stayed awake for three hours in the silent darkness, rehearsing in his mind all the things he had heard this man from Galilee teach. The conflicts he wrestled with made his head burn and ache. The heart of the matter was that as strange as the doctrine Jesus espoused was, it fit so perfectly into what Joseph had always believed.

"I know," he said at last.

"You know what?" Devorah snapped.

"I know they talk of him as the long awaited Messiah. What's more, he refers to himself that way."

"Joseph!" she screamed, her eyes wide and burning with intensity. "You believe this man is the Messiah, don't you!" It was an accusation, not a question, and both of them knew it.

Joseph rested his elbows on the table in front of him and rubbed his eyes with his fingertips. He ran his hands through his graying hair and stroked his flowing beard. He was so weary. He churned her question in his mind. It was the same question he had asked himself countless times over the past few weeks—the same question that had robbed him of sleep last night.

He looked at Devorah through bloodshot eyes, knowing that his response would have far greater impact than either she or he could imagine. Denying Jesus would be the safest thing to do. Life for him would continue much as it had for the past several years. He would maintain his position in the Sanhedrin and continue as a respected member of Jewish society, plus his business would continue to provide immense wealth. And Devorah, his sweet wife, would remain by his side and continue to enjoy the way of life she had become accustomed to and so enjoyed.

Acknowledging Jesus as the Messiah meant certain expulsion from the Sanhedrin and, at best, a formal discipline by the rulers of the synagogue where he attended weekly Sabbath meetings. At worst, he would be excommunicated from the synagogue, and his friends, family, and Jews everywhere would likely turn their backs on him. He would be ostracized in the city, and his successful business would crumble for lack of customers. He'd still be able to maintain his relationships with the Greeks and other non-Jews, but he wouldn't earn a fraction of the money he now did. And Devorah—what would she do? Her Jewish faith was deep and abiding, drilled into her from her earliest days by her father until he died and also by a succession of aristocratic rabbis and priests and her cousin Caiaphas, the venerated high priest. What would she do?

Leaning back in the chair, he let his arms slump to his side. He gazed quietly at her and softly said, "I love you, Devorah."

The response was like throwing dry tinder on a fire. "You love me?" she fired back, her voice now choked with emotion. "You *love* me? How can you sit there and say those words, knowing how deeply your actions hurt me? And not only me, but our children and grandchildren as well."

Devorah turned her back to him and slammed the pot on the stone counter, shattering it into a hundred pieces and sending water flying. Without facing him, she said in very measured tones, "It can't be like this, Joseph. You must decide. It is either this Jesus or me, but you can't have both."

THREE

❖ ❖ ❖ ❖ ❖ ❖

Caiaphas, Simeon, and a small retinue of lesser priests plodded their way up the road toward the main entrance of the massive building. Aside from the occasional grumble over a stubbed toe, there was little conversation. A foul mood radiated from their leader, and anything more than a grunt or groan from someone in the group was met with an icy stare from his deep-set black eyes. The leader's gaunt face, with its high cheekbones and hawklike nose, only added to the intensity of the glare and caused the followers to look at the ground rather than at him or the massive structure that loomed on the road ahead of them.

Flinging his cloak over his shoulder, Caiaphas halted for the third time in less than a quarter mile, an unspoken signal that the entire group was to stop. Although there was an incline in the road, it was so slight it hardly merited attention, let alone a stop to catch his breath. Still, he stopped, sucked in a deep breath, held it momentarily, and slowly let it escape through his nose, causing a slight whistle as it went. Those who knew Caiaphas well—like Simeon, the second most powerful person in the Sanhedrin—understood that the stop and deep breath had nothing to do with the grade of the road. It had everything to do with controlling his anger.

The short pause allowed Caiaphas to subdue pent up emotion and gave time for his pulse to settle back to a more normal rate. More composed, he led the group the last hundred yards to the massive doors that sealed the entrance against riffraff and gawkers. As they neared, two Roman soldiers materialized from a small enclosure beside the doors. The late morning sun glistened off their shining body armor, and their bright red robes flowed behind them as each rapidly walked to the group with their swords drawn and shields at the ready.

"Who are you and what is your business here?" the taller and apparently senior man barked with self-appointed authority.

One of the lesser priests, Benjamin, scurried from his place at the back of the group and announced, "It is Caiaphas, the Nasi, and Simeon, the Av Beit Din of Jerusalem." Referring to Caiaphas and Simeon by their Jewish Sanhedrin titles, Benjamin expected the guards to bow in recognition, but instead they wrinkled their foreheads in confusion.

"Who?" the taller soldier asked, baffled.

Realizing their Jewish titles meant nothing to the soldier, Benjamin said with exasperation, "The chief high priest and vice chief justice of the Sanhedrin."

The guard glared at the men. He may not have recognized the men's names and Sanhedrin titles, and he couldn't have cared less about their function in Jewish society and religion, but he did know two things about the chief high priest. First, the man was a person the Jews held in high regard. Second, and most important to the guard, Caiaphas made life difficult for all soldiers by continually stirring the Jews up in rebellion against the Romans. The guard had never seen any of these men before, but he took an immediate dislike to all of them. Without saying anything more, he turned and walked to the massive doors and knocked loudly with the butt of his sword. A small portal opened in the door, and the guard began talking.

A moment later the portal closed, and the guard returned to where Caiaphas stood.

"You are to remain here," he broadcast to the entire group. Returning his sword to its scabbard, he and the other guard walked back to their small enclosure, leaving the group of priests standing awkwardly in the middle of the road, looking lamely at one another.

"Despicable Romans," Caiaphas said to Simeon as he adjusted the silken girdle that wrapped around his slender frame and held his robe in place.

Simeon smiled weakly but said nothing because of the distracted way in which Caiaphas made his remark. It was then that Simeon realized there was something other than the purpose of this trip annoying the chief high priest. "What's troubling you, Caiaphas?"

Caiaphas looked at his long-time associate and gave a slight smile. Simeon was perceptive. "It's Jesus. He is growing far too powerful and well known. We simply must do more to stop him."

"We're already doing much," Simeon responded.

Caiaphas dismissed the remark with a single shake of his head. "More, we must do more. And it's not only him, but anyone who sympathizes with him."

Their conversation was interrupted by the noise of one of the massive doors opening slightly. The guard emerged from his shelter, walked to the small crack, and exchanged a few words with the unseen person on the other side. Stepping away from the opening, he called out to the group. "Proceed."

The solid door opened only a little more, forcing the men to squeeze through the narrow passage one at a time. Caiaphas went first, his slight frame easily slipping through. Simeon was next, but he eyed the opening with trepidation. His ample girth would never fit through the small crack, so he called two lesser priests to come forward and pull the door wider. They struggled against the door's weight but moved it enough that Simeon could squeeze his way through. When the last man was inside, the door swung shut, although no one could see by whom or how it was done. The group was securely locked inside the Roman stronghold in Jerusalem, the Fortress of Antonia.

Inside the doors, a young man waited, his arms hanging limply at his side. He was dressed in a white tunic that hung to the middle of his thighs and was secured at his waist with a thin black leather belt tied in a knot. His arms and legs were thin, little more than skin draped over bones. The leather sandals on his feet were shoddy and well worn from walking countless footsteps each day around the massive fortress. He was a slave, his only crime being the misfortune of being a citizen from some forgotten country Rome had conquered during the past year.

The slave admired the richness of the men's apparel and instantly knew which one was the leader. Caiaphas's deep grey robe was made from elegantly soft wool. Its billowing cuffs were trimmed in silver, and it had a linen collar that was dark black. His multicolored cloak matched perfectly and was made without a seam. The conical turban he wore on his head was made of the finest black silk and trimmed in thin strands of gold. Simeon's robe and cloak bespoke wealth, and though less impressive than Caiaphas's, they were superior to any of the others. In other circumstances, the slave might have been even more awed by this display of costly apparel, but not today. It was food that occupied his mind. He hadn't been able to scrounge any food in two days, and he was hungry.

In an emotionless voice, he asked, "Who is the leader?" although he already knew.

"I am," Caiaphas responded, stepping forward.

"You are to follow me. Everyone else is to remain here."

Caiaphas shook his head slightly and pointed to Simeon.

"This man will accompany me." It was spoken as a directive, not a request.

The young slave shrugged his shoulders. He might get beaten for it later, but he really didn't care if the second man came. In fact he didn't care if they all wanted to come along; he just wanted them to hurry. It was nearing the middle of the day, and the sooner he could get the men to their destination, the sooner he could sneak to the ovens where other slaves would be baking bread. If he timed it right, he could steal a loaf and find an isolated spot to devour it and satisfy the hunger pangs in his stomach.

The slave started across the compound at a fast pace, far faster than Caiaphas could walk. "We must hurry," he called back to the two men.

Caiaphas had no intention of hurrying, neither for this slave nor for his master. He would walk at his own pace and arrive when he arrived. If they had to wait, so be it.

As they walked, Caiaphas admired the Roman structures. Although he would never admit it to anyone, every time he had been to the Roman fortress he was secretly impressed with the sheer grandeur of the place. The huge courtyard was an oasis, and depending upon the time of year, flowers were often in bloom while trees and benches dotted the landscape. Long colonnades provided breezeways around the entire perimeter, creating a beautiful space to walk. It was a fortress in every sense of the word, with battlements and housing for six hundred soldiers, but it was also a place of comfort and grandeur, and that struck a resonate chord in Caiaphas—he liked the finer things of life.

With constant prodding, the slave finally managed to get the two men across the courtyard and into the most impressive building on the perimeter. Passing through an open doorway, the threesome walked in silence down a long hallway that led to the inner sanctums of the building, which became more opulent with each step. It was obvious this was a place where privileged people lived, not soldiers. They suddenly stopped outside an ornate door, which had another slave standing beside it. This slave was not only better dressed but also better fed and apparently better educated. After a quick exchange of words, the first slave darted down a hallway and disappeared from sight.

"Please wait here," the new slave said courteously and slipped inside the door. Caiaphas and Simeon exchanged glances but said nothing. They had been here before and knew that they would be kept waiting. Caiaphas stepped across the hallway and examined a marble statue that stood in an alcove. It was new, something that had been added since he was last summoned.

The sculpture was almost life-size and depicted a woman standing in robes that flowed from her shoulders to bare feet. She stood permanently frozen in mid-stride, her weight on her left leg with her right leg slightly extended, as if taking a step forward. Long strands of hair curled loosely around her cheeks and down her back. Caiaphas noted that her delicate nose and mouth were perfectly sculpted, and that her eyes were hidden behind a sculpted scarf that encircled her head, its ends lost in the waves of hair on the back of her head. In her left arm she held several tablets with Grecian inscriptions. Her right arm extended upward, away from her body. Suspended from her hand was a balance, the kind used to measure weight. Caiaphas's eyes dropped to the base of the sculpture, where a bronze plaque bore a single word: "JUSTICE."

The opening of the door behind him caused Caiaphas to turn abruptly. "Follow me" the slave said, and he led the two men into a chamber. The room was large and exquisitely furnished with polished tile floors, marble and cedar walls, and a large fireplace that dominated one wall. Dozens of chairs and a few small couches had been thoughtfully arranged around the fireplace as well as the room's perimeter to create settings where numerous intimate conversations could take place at the same time. Eight tall windows lined one side of the room, their long red drapes pulled back to allow sunlight and the fresh spring breeze into the room. At the far end of the room was a dais, raised one step above the rest of the floor.

The three of them walked almost halfway across the room before the slave stopped abruptly. Centered on the dais sat a beautifully carved chair with a high back and arms. Gold and brilliantly colored gems were inlaid along the legs and sides of the chair, which rested on a plush woven rug, bleached snow white. The slave bowed deeply to the chair's occupant and retreated from the room without saying a word.

Caiaphas pulled his robe around him and stood still, his weight evenly distributed on both legs. He could think of no one he despised more than the man in this room, and he wasn't alone in his feelings. Virtually every Jew shared his disdain and contempt. To stand here and be subjected to his condescending attitude tested Caiaphas to the limit. But this meeting was important for him, as were all those which had occurred in the past, and he couldn't allow his feelings to get in the way.

"Welcome, Caiaphas," the man said slowly, the words dripping off his tongue like thick honey. Then with the slightest nod of his head, he added, almost as an afterthought, "And to you as well, Simeon."

"Jehovah with you, Pontius Pilate," replied Caiaphas, knowing his response would both irritate the man and reinforce that Caiaphas was subject to God, not this loathsome Roman procurator. In truth, the last thing Caiaphas wanted was his God to be with Pilate. Secretly he hoped Jehovah would strike the brutal and murderous man with some terrible disease, and if the disease could be long and painful, he would like it even more.

Caiaphas's dislike for the Roman was returned in kind.

Pilate hated the Jews. He hated their religion, their customs, and anything that had to do with them as a people. They were difficult, headstrong, and perpetually causing commotion by staging uprisings. They made life uncomfortable for him with his superiors in Rome, so he was happy to oppress them, or kill them, whenever he had the need or opportunity.

The two men looked at each other with equal distrust and animosity. In past years, this meeting would have been unnecessary. For untold generations when the Feast of the Passover, Feast of the Tabernacles, or other sacred Jewish festivals came, the high priest would purify himself, dawn his ornate purple robes, and preside in the synagogue and at celebrations attired in kingly fashion. Since the Romans had conquered Judea, though, they had become the keepers of the sacred robes. They would only allow the high priest to have them in his possession a few days before each feast and would collect them immediately afterwards. With Passover only days away, Caiaphas was there to obtain the robes.

The whole process was an insult, a deliberately calculated show of authority designed to remind the Jews that Rome was the supreme authority. It also served as a forceful reminder that Pilate was in control and that at any time he could execute all the members of the Sanhedrin at his whim. His predecessors had done it before, and he wouldn't hesitate to do it again if it resulted in keeping the peace or demonstrating his power. These Jews were free to worship their God, Pilate told himself, but they should never forget that this freedom was granted through the benevolence of Rome.

"I trust you have been well," Pilate said without emotion, swatting at a fly that darted about his balding head.

"Jehovah has been kind to me," Caiaphas responded without bothering to return the courtesy of asking about Pilate's health, which he hoped was poor.

Pilate looked intently at the Jewish high priest and said,

"Tell me, Caiaphas, what do you know about this teacher of yours, this man from Galilee who has the people so excited?"

The anger Caiaphas felt toward Rome suddenly rerouted itself. Although Pilate hadn't mentioned Jesus by name, they both knew exactly about whom he was speaking, and the mention of Jesus galled Caiaphas. Jesus had begun as a slight irritation to Caiaphas, an uncomfortable pebble in his sandal, but during the past three years, his influence and power had swelled, and Caiaphas now viewed him as an open and festering sore, a sore that needed to be cleaned. He swallowed hard and feigned a confused look on his face before innocently responding.

"Teacher? I don't know who you're talking about," Caiaphas said as he raised his hands to his chest and loosely gripped the edges of his cloak.

"Come, come, Caiaphas," Pilate said, waving his hand in disbelief. "The countryside is awash with his deeds. Even in Caesarea I have heard rumors of his miracles."

Caiaphas pretended to be lost in thought and finally said, "Ah, perhaps you're referring to Jesus of Nazareth. I know nothing of him; you seem to know more about him than I."

"I've heard reports that he is drawing away thousands of people from your synagogues," Pilate said, knowing his remarks would annoy the man.

"I know nothing of this, your Excellency," Caiaphas lied.

"Hmm," Pilate said, realizing he was not going to get any useful information from the high priest. Changing the subject, he said, "With the Feast of the Passover approaching, I have brought with me from Caesarea your ceremonial robes." He motioned toward a young woman who had entered the room behind Caiaphas. In her arms she held a large bundle tied with a snow-white cord, interlaced with strands of gold. The action was intended to annoy and upset Caiaphas, and it succeeded.

Caiaphas turned toward the woman, doing nothing to hide

his annoyance. These were priestly robes, robes that were to be touched only by those who held the priesthood. It was bad enough when pagan Roman men handled the robes, but now they were being held by an idol-worshipping Roman woman!

Without taking his eyes from the girl, he waved his right hand to Simeon. There was no need to say anything. Simeon was equally horrified and leaped toward the girl, retrieving the bundle.

Pilate leaned back in his chair, straightened his white cashmere robe, and smiled to himself, knowing his stunt had elicited the exact reaction he was hoping it would. With a faint smirk on his lips, Pilate said, "You may leave, Caiaphas. I shall send a centurion to retrieve the robes the day after your Passover feast."

Caiaphas waited for Simeon to return to his side. Spinning on their heels, the two men walked hurriedly out the door without uttering a word.

"Have the old man watched closely until after the Passover," Pilate said to the centurion who had slipped in a side door and was now standing at his side. "He knows far more than he lets on, and he's up to something. These late night meetings he's holding at his palace and the rumors we're hearing about how he's exciting the people against this Jesus suggest he might be planning a revolt." Bringing his two palms together for emphasis, he said, "I'll crush them all before I'll let that happen."

FOUR

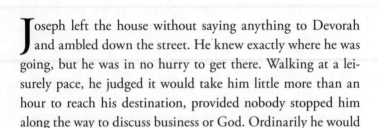

Joseph left the house without saying anything to Devorah and ambled down the street. He knew exactly where he was going, but he was in no hurry to get there. Walking at a leisurely pace, he judged it would take him little more than an hour to reach his destination, provided nobody stopped him along the way to discuss business or God. Ordinarily he would be eager to discuss either subject, but today he wanted time alone—time to think.

It was a pleasant walk. The late morning sun beat down on his shoulders with a warmth that said winter had finished its course and summer was coming. The biting wind that had annoyed him all winter and made his bones ache was now nothing more than a pleasant light breeze, gently stirring the palm fronds above his head as he walked along the street.

The scent of citrus blossoms wafted through the air as he walked down the broad, fashionable avenues that made up the upper city. Along its well-ordered grid of streets were the spacious homes—palaces really—of his wealthy neighbors. A wry smile creased his lips when he saw how each one tried to outdo the other with more elaborate gardens or reflecting pools. Joseph's wealth exceeded nearly all of theirs, but he didn't flaunt it. He lived in a spacious home, to be sure, and he had servants that attended to his and Devorah's every need, but he had always been cautious to distinguish needs from wants.

The sight of a young man struggling up a ladder with a load of bricks made Joseph stop. He had watched over the past months as stone masons had carefully constructed a sizeable addition to his neighbor's mansion. It looked beautiful, but Joseph wondered why old Uzza and his wife needed the extra room. They had no children or grandchildren, and it must be costing them plenty.

Displaying his wealth had never been important to Joseph. Perhaps it was a holdover from his boyhood years, when poverty kept food from his mouth. As hard as his father worked to provide for Joseph, his mother, and his four sisters, there was never enough. Far too young to work, the children scrounged from the garbage of the rich people and begged when wealthy merchants passed them on the streets. It was a pitiful existence, one where death brought relief.

Going to sleep at night in the small hut they called home, Joseph listened to the quiet whimpering of Sophia, his younger sister, as hunger pangs rumbled in her stomach. Joseph had stolen for her—many times. He would slip down the crowded streets of Arimathea, weaving between the shops of food merchants, and wait for the perfect opportunity. When an unsuspecting shop keeper turned his back or was busy helping a customer, Joseph would creep to the tables of fruit or vegetables, steal figs or pomegranates, and then run for home as fast as his bare feet would take him. Hiding the stolen morsels from his parents, for they would have been furious to know of his thievery, he would divide it among his sisters, giving Sophia a double portion.

In the end it wasn't enough. Sophia died with a bloated belly, a victim of starvation. He never understood how someone could starve to death, yet still have a large stomach. For months after Sophia's death, whenever he saw a fat person walking down the streets of Arimithea, he felt sorrow for the person, believing their well-fed body was showing signs of imminent death. Within three years, two more sisters died, one of hunger and the other of some unknown illness his mother's remedies couldn't cure. A year later, his father died, his body worn out and riddled with illness.

At thirteen, Joseph faced a decision: starve with his mother and remaining sister, or leave home to find work. He chose to leave. Lying about his age, he found thankless work on a ship bound for Tarshish. Joseph worked tirelessly and willingly at every task, regardless of how grimy, difficult, or dangerous. While others complained, Joseph complied, and his actions didn't go unnoticed by the ship's owner. Sensing in Joseph a keen mind and willing heart, he gave Joseph greater responsibilities and greater privileges. He taught Joseph to read and write and eventually made it possible for him to buy his own small fishing boat when he was seventeen. The income from that boat enabled him to snatch his mother and sister from starvation's door.

Over the next five years, Joseph worked, scrimped, and saved enough to purchase a small sailing ship. Slow and leaky, Joseph used it to haul merchandise between small ports no one else wanted to visit. In time, a second ship was acquired, larger and not so leaky, and Joseph expanded his trade routes to more profitable places. Eventually, Joseph had a fleet of ships and a trading business that extended throughout the Great Sea. Shrewd, determined, and willing to take risks, Joseph grew into a wealthy man over the years, a man who loved God and his neighbor.

With the fear of poverty burned deeply in his soul, Joseph learned to make do with what he had. It was either that or go without, which he did on so many occasions he no longer kept track. Even today, when he could afford to purchase anything he wanted, he still asked himself if he really needed it. More often than not the answer was no, so he didn't buy.

Joseph's thrifty nature caused Devorah some irritation in their early years of marriage and even now could cause contention. She was not extravagant, but she wasn't afraid to spend money. "If you're not going to spend it, you might as well be accumulating rocks," she once told him. She was right, of course, but it was difficult for him to spend money—at least on himself. He was always willing and often gave money to those in need. Without fanfare, he had supported scores of widows and had been generous in supplying the needs of countless orphans. He had provided handsomely for each of his four children, all sons, and he would be certain his grandchildren were taken care of equally well.

No, Joseph thought as he watched the stone masons work, there were better things he could do with his wealth than build a monument to himself in the form of a large palace or mansion, and he continued his walk.

Thirty minutes after leaving the gates of his estate, he'd exchanged the ordered cleanliness of the upper city for the squalor of the lower city. Its maze of dusty streets and cramped alleyways meandered uphill and down in every direction. The peaceful serenity of the upper city was replaced by the mad rush of people jostling and screaming at one another as they eked out a living.

Joseph watched as a donkey with merchandise piled high and wide on its back obediently followed a man working his way through the throng. The little beast was barely visible beneath its load, which swayed precariously with each step.

"Out of the way! Big load!" the man called in warning to Joseph.

Joseph jumped sideways against a fence to avoid being hit and watched as the man and donkey passed. Two goats bleated loudly from behind the fence and immediately began nibbling on a portion of his robe that was between the slats. Stepping away from the fence, Joseph pulled his robe from the goats and gazed down the street ahead of him. The scene was not inviting.

Shepherds leading sheep, men on camels, and more donkeys loaded with goods competed with mobs of people for space in the congested mess. And the worst part, Joseph thought, was that he hadn't yet reached the marketplace, which was sure to be even more crowded. Considering what lay before him, Joseph decided to take an alternate route. It was more roundabout and would add a few extra minutes to his walk, but it would allow him to avoid the mass of people and animals before him as well as most of the street vendors hawking everything from cheap trinkets to food.

Joseph turned down a narrow alleyway and walked briskly past some hovels with raw sewage in front of them. The alley emptied onto a street that, although crowded, was nowhere near as congested as where he had been. Passing rows of two-story houses, he turned up another alley so narrow that the houses on each side blocked the sun. Even though it was late morning, it was dark and dismal. In the faint light, he could see dirty children dressed in rags playing in the dirt. The sight didn't shock or offend him; he'd seen far worse.

Leaving the alley, he stepped onto a wide street that ran beside the great temple and although he shouldn't have been, he was startled at what he saw. Passover was still a week away, yet greedy merchants were already vying for places to sell sheep, doves, and even sparrows to penitents who would come to offer sacrifice. He hated the atmosphere surrounding the temple this time of the year. It offended his sensibility and flew in the face of what he believed God intended the sacred festival of Passover to be. Joseph pushed his way through the crowds, ignoring the men and women trying to sell him sacrificial animals.

Several minutes later he arrived at his destination, a beautiful garden just outside the walls of the temple. The solitude and serenity were normally a welcome relief from the hustle and bustle behind him, but now he was assaulted by something entirely different, something he enjoyed even less.

Walking along the path toward the entrance of the garden, the unwelcome but now familiar sense of foreboding settled over him. It was the same every time he visited the tomb. In the beginning, he stopped by the tomb once or twice a week to check on the stone hewer's progress, but as the work progressed, so did a sense of despair. The sadness left him so unnerved that he lengthened the time between visits until he simply stopped coming at all. In fact, he hadn't visited the spot in weeks, and it was only after receiving a message from the stone hewer, telling him the tomb was completed that he forced himself to make the trip. Now he unconsciously slowed his pace to delay the flood of sadness that would inevitably assault him upon nearing the tomb.

It had been three years since the impression first came to him to have a tomb hewn from the stone cliff in the garden. The first time the thought came, he pushed it from his mind, fearful that it was a precursor to his impending death, or worse, Devorah's or one of his grandchildren's. Over the next year, the impression came more frequently and strongly until it grew impossible to ignore, so he finally contacted the stone hewer.

Their first conversation was casual and without commitment. The stone hewer's questions were straightforward: Where was the tomb to be constructed? What dimensions would it be? How elaborate did he want it? And, of course, how was he to be paid? These were questions Joseph hadn't considered, and he was unprepared to answer them, so they concluded the conversation with Joseph telling the man he would let him know if and when he wanted to proceed.

Months passed and he'd done nothing further, almost succeeding in pushing thoughts of the tomb from his mind. Then, one night, he awoke suddenly from a disturbing dream.

Actually, Devorah had awoken him because he was thrashing about in the bed and rambling incoherently in his sleep about death and tombs.

Almost two years had passed since he had the first impression, and not once in that time had he said a word to his wife about constructing a tomb. For all her goodness, Devorah had a tendency to overreact. Small piles of dirt could turn into mountains the size of Ararat in the blink of an eye. But now there was no avoiding it. That night after she shook him from his sleep, while trying to comfort and console him, she persisted in learning the details of his dream. His vague answers only heightened her curiosity, and in the end, he told her everything—not only the details of the dream, but the constant stream of impressions that had come to him during the past years.

To his complete amazement, Devorah was understanding and even encouraged him to have the tomb hewn. When he expressed his surprise at her reaction, she said she had been feeling the same way for the past several months but had been afraid to say anything. Like Joseph, she didn't understand why the impressions were coming, but she viewed them as a sign from God, and that was enough for her. Her positive response was enough for Joseph. Early the next morning, he contracted with the stone hewer to construct the tomb.

Joseph unlatched the gate, entered the garden, and was overcome by its beauty. The buds on trees had burst into leaves, and now blossoms were beginning to show their delicate flowers. The grass that lined the stone walk had changed from the yellow of winter to the bright green of spring. Sparrows chirped noisily and fluttered from tree to tree while the mournful cooing of doves echoed all around him. Were he here for a different purpose, he probably could have enjoyed the sights, sounds, and smells. As it was, he walked forward with trepidation.

Joseph casually acknowledged the gardener and his young assistant as they labored to cut a dead limb from an ancient olive tree that had crashed to the ground during a recent storm. He wandered silently toward the tomb, wondering how far he would get before the morose feelings would settle over his mind and heart.

Rounding a final bend in the trail, Joseph saw the tomb. The rectangular entrance through which he had crawled on past visits was now partially blocked by a massive stone that would ultimately be used to seal the entrance. The stone was rounded and stood slightly askew, revealing only a small portion of the tomb's entrance at the upper and lower corners. The stone had been there weeks before, but then it was little more than an odd-shaped lump and it hadn't been blocking the entrance.

Joseph stopped a short distance from the stone and stared at its rough surface. How many blows with a chisel, he wondered, had it taken to shape the stone so it could be rolled? More important, he thought as he looked at the huge stone, how was he ever going to move it by himself so he could get inside. He smiled and wondered if this stone slab was a blessing in disguise. Although he wanted to examine the inside of the tomb, he dreaded the morose feelings he'd experienced whenever he entered it in the past. Now with the massive stone blocking the entrance, he had a convenient excuse to avoid going inside.

Joseph took the last few steps to the stone and stopped, waiting for the sense of foreboding to descend upon him as it had every time in the past. To his surprise it didn't come. Instead, there was a strange sense of relief, almost a calm peaceful feeling. Puzzled and confused, he stepped closer, as if there was some connection between his proximity to the tomb and the intensity of the emotion—but there was no morose sadness, no gloomy feeling, only a peaceful sense of relief.

Reaching out his hand, he ran his fingers over the stone's

surface. Without thinking, he stepped to the side of the stone and, laying his shoulder against its rough edges, attempted to push it out of the way. Nothing! Turning his back to the stone he squatted down, letting out a deep breath. Then he heaved against the mass of rock with all his strength, but again there was no movement. Sighing, he told himself he shouldn't be surprised. "It would take three strong men to move this stone," he mumbled.

With no feelings of sadness to plague him, Joseph was determined to look inside. Dropping to his stomach, he managed to wriggle his left arm, shoulder, and head into the small opening at the bottom corner. A shaft of bright sunlight streaked through the small opening at the upper corner of the entrance and pierced the darkness inside. Joseph's eyes slowly adjusted from the light of the garden to the dark of the tomb. He shook his head in disbelief. He had expected to see roughly hewn walls with sharp, jagged edges of rock jutting out incongruously while the stone ledge, which would be the final resting place for the body, would be only slightly smoother.

Even in the semi-darkness, he could see that not only the walls but also the ceiling and floor were smooth. Not as smooth as polished marble, but smooth enough that someone could lay, sit, or lean virtually anywhere without undo discomfort. He was amazed at the progress that had been made since his last visit.

Wanting a better and more comfortable view, Joseph withdrew from the opening. Laying flat on his stomach and pushing mightily with his toes he managed to wriggle both arms, his head, and a portion of his shoulders into the small opening for a better look. It was an unwise move. He could see even less, and now he was unable to move either forward or backward. He was stuck. Momentary panic set in, and he was about to scream when he heard the footfalls of people running.

"Counselor, are you well?" said the voice, calling Joseph by his Sanhedrin title.

"No, I'm stuck!" Joseph cried out as he tried again to inch out of his predicament. The words had scarcely left his lips when a pair of hands grabbed each of his legs and tugged, pulling him backwards out of the opening. Lying awkwardly on his stomach, Joseph turned to look up into the faces of the gardener and his helper.

"Thank you for your help," Joseph said, rising to his feet and brushing dust from his robe. With a slightly embarrassed tone, he added, "I am Joseph of Arimathea."

"I know, sir," said the man, bowing deeply at the waist. "Zophar, the stone hewer, and I have had many conversations about this tomb and who commissioned it."

Joseph raised an eyebrow but said nothing.

"It is without a doubt the finest tomb in the garden, and we," he said, motioning with his calloused hand toward his assistant, "have watched its construction with interest. Never would I have imagined this spot in the garden would yield such beautiful stone. Would you like help in moving the entrance stone so you can walk inside?"

The question caught Joseph off guard and he hesitated.

"Forgive me, Counselor, but you should see what it looks like inside," the gardener said. It was more of a command than a statement, and he stepped past Joseph up to the stone. "Come, boy, push with all your might," he said sternly to his assistant. The heavily muscled youth squatted down and placed his back against the stone while the gardener stood above him and pushed with his shoulder. Together the two of them strained. The heavy stone moved but almost imperceptibly.

Joseph immediately saw the problem. The stone hewer had masterfully cut the channel in which the stone rolled at a slight slope. One or two men could easily roll the stone down the gradual slope and into the final resting place to seal the tomb, but opening the tomb meant rolling the stone up the incline.

"Is that the best you can do?" the old man barked at the youth. "Push or I'll send you back to live with the rats!"

Taking a deep breath and letting out an explosive yell, the young man heaved against the stone. This time there was more movement, but it was instantly obvious the two of them wouldn't succeed, so Joseph sprang to their aid. With legs and arms straining, the three of them managed an odd rhythm that got momentum on their side. The stone moved first a few inches and then a foot before the exhausted assistant collapsed to the ground, his strength entirely wasted. As he fell, the stone came to a stop, far too heavy for the two old men to continue moving on their own, and it threatened to roll back down the slope.

"Hurry!" the gardener yelled to his assistant. "Find something to keep the stone from rolling back."

The young assistant rose on trembling legs, picked up a rock the size of his fist, and wedged it in place so the stone couldn't roll.

Joseph and the gardener cautiously relaxed their hold on the stone and stepped back, waiting to see if it would roll over the rock. Satisfied it was secure, Joseph wiped his hand on his robe and extended it so he could shake hands with the gardener and the assistant. "Thank you," he said sincerely. "There isn't any way I could have done that by myself."

"You're welcome," the gardener said as he and his assistant moved away from the entrance to allow Joseph enough room to squeeze through.

Tiny dust particles swirled in commotion as sunlight streamed through the opening and bounced off the rocky surfaces, allowing Joseph to see clearly, but dimly, every portion of the tomb. Shuffling first to one side and then the other, for he could not stand completely upright in the tomb, he ran his hands along the almost smooth walls. The rock was cool, almost cold. Withdrawing his hand, Joseph looked at his fingers, expecting them to be coated with dust, but there was none. The walls had been wiped clean of any residue from the construction.

Joseph was deeply impressed as he looked around the room. The stone hewer had taken Joseph's vague instructions and expanded on them dramatically, creating a work of art in the process. An intricate arch had been carved into each wall that gave the appearance of a window. Beneath each arch, a small ledge had been chiseled to create a shelf. These shelves, Joseph knew, would hold ornate urns and vases to decorate the tomb. Delicate flowers had been chiseled into each wall just above the floor and gave the impression that they were growing out of the floor. High on the wall, above where the dead person's head would rest, the stonecutter had chiseled a sun with rays streaming out from it.

It was more than what Joseph had anticipated. This, Joseph said to himself, was a tomb fit for a king.

Turning about, Joseph faced the stone ledge that would ultimately be the resting place for the body and stared for a long minute. "Whose body will lie here?" he quietly said aloud. "For whom has this tomb been constructed?"

With that thought hanging in his mind, he stepped over to the ledge and sat down. As if pressed with a weight, his shoulders slumped forward, and an involuntary sigh oozed from his lungs. Folding his hands in his lap, he quietly uttered, "For whom is this tomb?"

FIVE

Nicodemus absentmindedly eyed the water in the cup in his hand. The seventy-five-year-old man rotated the earthen cup round and round, swirling the water in circles. He was trying to see how close to the brim he could get it without spilling any. It was an absentminded action, something a youth would do, not a member of the Sanhedrin with a graying beard and portly stomach.

He chastised himself as several drops sloshed over the edge and landed on the papyrus manuscript lying on his wooden desk. He quickly brushed the errant drops from the sacred roll with the back of his hand. Wiping his hand on his robe, he looked discreetly around the chamber to see if any of his fellow council members had noticed. None had. Breathing a sigh of relief, he inconspicuously fanned the spots where the water drops had landed in an effort to accelerate their drying. As the spots faded and disappeared, he again chastised himself for not paying attention to what Simeon was saying. His mind continually returned to the verbal exchange he had had the previous night with the man from Galilee, the man known as Jesus.

He had gone to visit Jesus secretly at night, hiding under the protective blanket of darkness as he had during his three previous visits. Although he admired and believed the words the man spoke, he was much too controversial, and Nicodemus had too much to lose if seen in his presence. After all, half of the people sitting in the Sanhedrin this very moment were outwardly hostile to Jesus and schemed to destroy him. They wanted him silenced and were doing everything they could to pressure the other half of the council to agree with them.

He could readily accept this man from Galilee and his teachings—privately, not openly. Publicly associating with the man could cost Nicodemus his position in the Sanhedrin, his status as a respected teacher of the law, and his highly regarded position in society. He loved his lifestyle, the stately home in which he lived, people bowing to him as he walked down the street, and people constantly seeking his opinion on matters of not only Jewish law but doctrine as well. It was a good life, one he was unwilling to sacrifice on the altar of conscience.

Nicodemus looked again at the water in the cup. He was a man divided. The teachings of Jesus rang true to his heart, but the more he contemplated them, the more conflicted he became. Jesus had summed up his feelings perfectly last week when he said, "A man cannot serve two masters." The statement struck Nicodemus forcefully and instantly made him wonder how he was going to meld his life as a Pharisee with being a believer in Jesus.

It was his wife, Anna, who introduced him to the doctrine of Jesus many months before. She and two servants had first encountered him weeks before when she went to the marketplace for her daily food purchases. She had haggled over the price of bread with the baker, purchased several varieties of nuts from some Ishmaelite traders, and when she could no longer withstand the constant badgering by a young boy following her down the street, she bought a small bag of his dried dates. Her final stop was to buy melons before returning to her estate.

Although her servants grumbled, she insisted on buying the

melons from a particular merchant. "We walk past ten other merchants selling melons before we get to Haichim's stand," they murmured, "and their melons are every bit as sweet and juicy." It wasn't just the added distance that caused the servants to complain; it was also the location. His stand was down a small alley, which even under the best of circumstances, was jammed with people, and because the Feast of the Tabernacle was so near, the crowd would be shoulder to shoulder. Pushing their way through the mass of people with arms loaded full of food would be difficult, but Anna dismissed the servants' grumbling with the wave of a hand and plunged into the ocean of people crowding the alley.

Pushing her way to Haichaim's stand, she stood under the awning, touching and smelling melons, trying to decide exactly which would be the most flavorful.

"Excellent choice!" the short, stocky shopkeeper called out to Anna as she rotated a musk melon in her hand. "It just arrived this morning on a caravan. Very sweet! Perfect flavor!"

Anna eyed him warily, knowing he wasn't above stretching the truth to make a sale. "How much?" she shouted above the competing voices in the shop.

Before he could reply, Anna was distracted by a commotion near the end of the alley. That was the first time she saw Jesus. Surrounded by an even thicker mob of people than lined the alley around her, he slowly pushed his way in her direction.

It was his soft radiance that made her stare. Not a bright light or glow but something that emanated calm, peace, and a spirit she had never before seen. He simply stood out from the mass of people around him. Although it was hot, an involuntary shiver raced down her spine, causing her shoulders to tremble. Some of those nearest him were trying to keep the people away to give him room to walk, but it was useless. There were simply too many people clamoring for his attention.

As Anna stepped from under the awning to get a better

look, she was shoved violently from behind. A pitifully poor young man, dressed in a tattered and torn robe, forced his way past her, clutching a bundle to his chest that was wrapped in a filthy piece of goatskin. Pushing through the rows of people until he stood directly in front of Jesus, he stopped, his body blocking any forward movement. He tenderly unwrapped the goatskin to reveal a hideously deformed infant. Her arms were little more than stumps; her swollen, misshaped head was the size of the melon Anna held in her hands; and her left foot protruded from her leg at a strange angle. Anna gasped in horror at the sight of the baby and involuntarily turned her head, covering her mouth to squelch the rising bile in her throat.

In a single smooth gesture, the man bowed deeply at the waist, his eyes to the ground, and extended his arms to their full length, proffering the baby to Jesus. He stood there, bowed in silence, no words passing his lips.

To Anna, it was as if time stood still. The incessant noise of buyers and sellers haggling over wares simply faded from her hearing. Jesus stopped and looked at the man who held the baby in trembling hands. Then he slowly turned his head, sweeping his gaze over the mass of people packed into the narrow alleyway. Looking from one to another, he examined the faces of the crowd as if searching for a particular person. Then he looked in Anna's direction. At first she thought he was looking at her, but then she realized his gaze was locked on the frail young woman who had materialized at her side.

Anna judged the woman to be sixteen or seventeen, certainly no more than eighteen. She wore a torn, dirty, dark brown robe woven of coarse wool that had bits of straw and goat dung clinging to it. Her hair was matted with dirt, and her hands and feet were grimy. She looked emaciated and starving—everything about her screamed destitution.

Tears streamed down her dirty cheeks, leaving little trails of clean skin in their path, and she bit her lower lip in a vain effort to stop its quivering. But her eyes—they riveted Anna's attention—were dark, almost black, like the eyes of virtually every Jewish girl, but there was something more in them, profoundly more. There was a yearning, a pleading, an intensity that said, "I know you can, if only you will."

It was at that moment that Anna realized she was standing beside the mother of the little baby, who was now crying from the outstretched arms of a humble and believing father.

Anna watched as Jesus looked into the eyes of the young mother and nodded his head. It was an almost imperceptible tilt, nothing more than a single up and down motion. But Anna saw it and knew that the woman standing beside saw it as well. It was an acknowledgement, a confirmation that he both knew who she was and clearly understood her unspoken request. But more than that, the nod conveyed approval of the young mother's absolute faith.

Tenderly, Jesus reached out his hands and took the small child from the outstretched arms of the father. Dropping the soiled goatskin to the ground, he cuddled the little baby in his arms and kissed her softly on the forehead to soothe her whimpering cries. Then, holding the baby in his left arm, he removed the finely woven shawl from around his shoulders and gently wrapped it around the baby girl. Bowing his head to where his lips almost touched the child's head, he uttered words that were lost in the din of the crowd. Raising his head, Jesus looked at the young woman beside Anna and walked toward her.

As he stopped in front of her, he smiled but said nothing to the young mother. Handing her the baby, still wrapped in his shawl, he turned away and continued walking up the alley. The young mother hugged the baby to her breast, grateful to have her back but feeling no urgency to peek beneath the shawl, for she knew. It was only after her husband was at her side and Jesus was well beyond them that together they removed the shawl.

Had Anna not been standing next to the woman, she would never have believed what she saw. As the mother gingerly uncovered the baby, she gazed down upon a perfectly formed little body. Arms, hands, feet, and head all exactly as they should be. Nothing misshapen. Nothing out of place.

"It's a miracle! The child is healed!" screamed an old woman who stood near the young couple. And then a dozen people started pushing and shoving in an effort to catch a glimpse of the baby. Jesus continued moving forward with the crowd, but when he was thirty or forty feet beyond the couple, he turned to look at them. They met his gaze, but Anna imagined it would have been difficult for them to see him clearly through the tears of gratitude that gushed from their eyes. The husband looked down at his wife and tiny daughter and encircled them in his arms. Together the couple reverently looked at Jesus and mouthed a silent thank-you.

Anna and the young couple watched in silence as Jesus made his way up the alley and rounded the corner. The couple admired their perfect little girl, and Anna admired them. That's when Anna did something she had never done before: she gave them food. She was simply overcome with a desire to help them and the only thing she could think to do was offer them food. At first the couple refused, too startled by the offer to accept it, but it was only a mild protest. Not only had she urged they take the food she had just purchased, but Anna also insisted that her servants go back to the marketplace, purchase additional food, and deliver it to the young family's crude shack.

That night, as Anna and Nicodemus sat on their veranda eating melons and dates, she related everything she had witnessed. Nicodemus listened in complete silence, more than a little surprised. After more than fifty years of marriage, he thought he'd seen every side of his wife, but she was talking and behaving like a stranger. While she had always been tolerant of poor people, never had he known her to be overly sentimental or show much compassion. For Nicodemus, the change was as heartwarming as it was surprising.

The very next day, Anna sought out Jesus and found him preaching outside the walls of the temple. She listened intently to everything he said and went away that day a true believer. It had taken her very little effort to convince Nicodemus, who was so amazed and pleased at the change in his wife, that he should listen to this man from Galilee.

After their first meeting, Nicodemus was convinced that Jesus was a teacher sent from God. He couldn't accept him as the long promised Messiah, as many of his followers did, but there was indeed something special about the man. At their third meeting, Nicodemus posed some questions that swayed his feelings.

"Rabbi," he had said to Jesus, "I know you're a teacher who has come from God. I've seen and heard of the miracles you've performed, and I know no man could perform such signs if God were not with him." Nicodemus paused briefly to formulate the question. "What must I do to be part of the kingdom of God?"

Jesus smiled and declared, "I'll tell you a truth; no one can see the kingdom of God unless he is born again."

"Surely a man can't be born when he is old," Nicodemus replied. "How can a man enter a second time into his mother's womb?"

"He can't," Jesus replied, "but he can be born of the water and of the Spirit. You must be born again or you can't gain eternal life. You must be baptized and given the Holy Spirit by one having authority."

"Baptism?" Nicodemus said, shaking his head. This was hard doctrine. Although the words had a ring of truth, they were at odds with the things he'd been taught since childhood. As a Pharisee, he believed in eternal life and resurrection, but this ordinance of baptism Jesus spoke about was new. He'd have to wrestle with the concept. Over the next several days Nicodemus had done exactly that, reconciled the concept of baptism, but now he was sorting his way through accepting Jesus as the Messiah—a much more difficult task.

Nicodemus was jolted back from his mental wanderings when he realized it was no longer Simeon's monotone voice he heard resounding through the chamber but that of Caiaphas, the chief priest.

"What of this man Jesus Christ?" he bellowed as he rose from the overstuffed chair on which he had been half reclining.

The question wasn't directed at him or anyone in particular, but it captured the attention of all the members of the Sanhedrin gathered in the room. Then the shouting began.

"He's a usurper of power! He's dangerous," cried out an ancient rabbi who was propped up in his chair with pillows.

"He's worse than that! He speaks blasphemy," shouted another. "He claims he is the Son of God."

"Aren't we all?" shouted a third, his response less in answer to the question than an indication of his indifference on the matter.

Across the room, two others shouted almost in unison, "He speaks wisely and knows the words of Jehovah."

This debate had raged several times before, always at Caiaphas's prodding, and it bitterly divided the Sanhedrin. Nicodemus blocked out the din and looked to where Caiaphas stood. He could see the slightest smile crease the old man's face as he surveyed the commotion, and Nicodemus wondered what ulterior, sinister motives lurked behind the smile.

Nicodemus switched his gaze across the room to his old friend Joseph of Arimathea. The two of them had had many conversations about their respective beliefs in Jesus, and Nicodemus was anxious to see Joseph's reaction. Joseph sat in his overstuffed chair, his arms folded loosely across his chest. Nicodemus could see that Joseph too was observing not only

Caiaphas, but each of the other council members as if making a mental tally of who spoke in favor and who spoke against Jesus.

Other than his wife, his three sons and their wives, and his two daughters and their husbands, Joseph was the only person who knew of Nicodemus's meetings with Jesus, and he wanted to keep it that way. Let the arguments rage and the debates ensue, Nicodemus had no intentions of doing or being anything but a quiet believer, someone who stands on the sidelines. But what about Joseph, Nicodemus wondered to himself. Would he actively support or remain a silent believer in Jesus?

SIX

Jehovah with you," Joseph said as he entered the door of the man who hewed tombs out of stone.

"Jehovah bless thee," the burly man responded, looking up from the stone slab that lay in front of him.

The familiar greeting was one the children of Israel had used for hundreds of years, and it cut across all class lines. Wealthy merchant or humble hewer of stone, one always invoked the blessings of Jehovah before anything else was said.

Joseph looked around the well-kept shop. It was small and cramped but tidy and well organized. Mallets, chisels, and other devices hung from pegs in the brick and mortar walls in orderly rows, neatly arranged by size. A white linen curtain, the only attempt to give the shop a homey look, hung limply over the window.

"Zophar, I've come to settle with you for your work," Joseph said, smiling. I've been to the garden; the tomb is remarkable. As excellent as your reputation is as a stone worker, it doesn't do you justice," Joseph said with complete sincerity.

The stone hewer placed his mallet and chisel on the stone and walked to where Joseph stood. He smiled at the compliment and said in a soft, unhurried voice, "You approve, then? It's what you wanted?"

"Oh, I completely approve. It's far more than I expected."

"Please, sit," Zophar said, motioning to a simple wooden chair beside an equally plain table. Walking to the opposite end of the table, he lowered himself into another chair and waited while Joseph sat down.

Joseph expected the man to speak, but instead he sat silently for a long moment, as if contemplating exactly what to say and how to say it. The man's long black beard had tiny flecks of marble stuck in it. His massive arms and barrel chest strained the seams of his sweat-soaked tunic. Using the leather armlet that encircled his left forearm, the stonemason wiped the sweat away from his forehead.

Leaning forward in his chair, Zophar rested a hand on each knee. "Never have I worked on a tomb such as that," he finally said in a soft voice, hardly more than a whisper.

The reverence with which he said it took Joseph by surprise. It was almost incongruous, this big hulk of a man speaking in soft tones. In their previous meetings, he had never been loud or boisterous, but now he was almost solemn when he spoke. Wrinkling his forehead and shifting his body in the unstable chair, Joseph asked, "What do you mean?"

There was no response for another long moment. "The stone, it cut perfectly. It was almost as if I had but to think how I wanted it to split and it happened. There were no fissures, no splinters, no inferior rock, and no mistakes." And then with great emphasis, he added, "It is *perfect* in every detail. It is fit for a king."

Taking a deep breath and slowly expelling it through slightly pursed lips, he continued, "The deeper into the rock I worked, the more beautiful the stone became. In fact, do you see those stones piled in the corner there?" he asked, pointing with his oversized hand to a pile of stone in the corner of the small shop. "They all came from the tomb. I will save them for cutting special markers." He grinned, having already calculated the premium price the stone would fetch.

Looking Joseph in the eye, he repeated, "The tomb is perfect in every respect. None more so. Even those carved in the Tomb of the Kings can't compare," Zophar said proudly.

It wasn't an altogether idle boast. The Tomb of the Kings in the lower level of Jerusalem's temple had been used for centuries as the final resting places for Judah's long line of kings. King David's tomb was there, as were dozens of others. Upon the death of a king, artisans skillfully crafted a tomb, making each slightly more ornate than the previous. Having been to the Tomb of the King's on several occasions, Joseph knew that Zophar's work rivaled any of them.

"It's interesting you should say that," Joseph said. "I thought it fit for a king myself."

A satisfied smile creased the burly stone hewer's face. "I created it with that purpose in mind," he said.

Joseph looked at him in puzzlement. "What do you mean?" Joseph asked.

Zophar paused and considered whether to say something more. Looking into Joseph's eyes, he said, "I am not a deeply religious man, but all my life I have been waiting to build this tomb."

"*This* tomb? Why?" Joseph asked, his confusion obvious.

Zophar nodded as he lifted his hands from his knees, intertwined his fingers together, and placed them on the table in front of him. "My father was a carpenter, and as his oldest son, I was expected to become one as well," he said. "As a child I ran around his shop, always trying to help, but mostly getting in his way. I loved working with my father. But when I turned thirteen, I had a dream. I dreamt I was a stone hewer."

Joseph gave a look of encouragement and waited for Zophar to continue.

"In my dream, I learned that I was destined for something more than just working with wood—I had a very special mission in life. I dreamt of a man I had never seen before, and he would ask me to hew a tomb for a king." There was a long pause, then Zophar added slowly and deliberately, "*You* were that man."

Joseph rocked back in surprise. "Me?" he asked in astonishment.

Zophar nodded once. "You. Not many days after my dream, my father died unexpectedly. Although I was considered a man at thirteen, I hadn't learned all the skills necessary to be a carpenter and continue with my father's shop. Neither I nor my mother knew it, but my father had debts when he died. His creditors demanded payment, and the only way we could satisfy the debt was if my mother sold his tools. We did so, but that left me with nothing to earn a living. My father's brother took our family in. He was a stone hewer, and although he was not a very good one, I began learning a new trade—his trade."

"But how does all this relate to me and building a tomb for a king?" Joseph questioned.

Zophar leaned back in his chair and folded his arms across his chest. "I don't know," he said with some bewilderment. "We Jews haven't had a king for hundreds of years, but all I know is that in my dream, I was told I would build a tomb for a king, and you were the man who would ask me to build it," Zophar replied.

Joseph sat back in his chair, stunned by what he had just been told. Just as it made no sense to Zophar, it made no sense to Joseph.

"Do you remember when you first came to my shop and inquired about a tomb?"

"Yes," Joseph said, nodding his head. "I left without contracting with you to build it."

"You did, and that surprised me. Even after all these years, when you walked through the door of my shop, I instantly recognized you as the man in my dream. As we talked, it was as if I had experienced everything once before; you, me, the surroundings, our conversation—everything was exactly as I had experienced it in my dream. When you left without asking me to do it, I went home to my wife and told her of your visit and how you left. She told me to be patient and that you would return. It took longer than I thought, but you came back."

Joseph and Zophar looked at each other, each lost in his own thoughts. After several minutes passed in confused silence, and not knowing what to say, Joseph reached inside his cloak and extracted a smooth leather pouch and emptied its contents on the table. The gold and silver coins rattled against the wood and one another as they landed and rolled around the table.

Zophar looked at the coins and sifted through them with his index finger and mentally tallied their value. "That's more than the agreed price," he said, looking up at Joseph.

"I know. But the work you did is far more than I expected and you deserve to be paid extra," Joseph said, rising from the chair.

"Thank you for your generosity, Counselor, but I only want what we agreed." Zophar sorted the coins into two stacks. Sliding the smaller stack of coins across the table, he said, "That tomb will yet be a blessing to me and my family."

Knowing there would be no way he could convince Zophar to take more money, Joseph picked up the coins one by one, dropped them into the bag, and pulled the drawstrings of the bag tightly. He tucked the pouch inside his robe and extended his hand to Zophar. "And the tomb will be a blessing to my family as well. Thank you," he said.

Zophar rose to his feet and clasped the outstretched hand. "You're welcome. And may God be with you in whatever lies in your future."

SEVEN

Dressed as he was, it would have been difficult to detect his nationality in the dark of night. At a quick glance, most people would have taken him for just another Jew, which is exactly what he was attempting to be. But in daylight or by the close light of a candle, any observer would have noticed too many differences.

All Jewish men had beards, but even the worst of them weren't as thin as his. It was scraggly and unkempt, and tonight it was slightly matted with fish oil and tiny crumbs of bread near the corners of his mouth, leftovers from his hurried noonday meal. Although he attempted to hide it under his scarf, his hair was too short and the wrong color. It barely covered the tops of his ears; Jewish men, especially those of his age, wore their hair longer, almost to their shoulders. And it was a light shade of brown rather than the deep brown or black of most Jews. Fortunately for him, his clothing was authentic and helped in the charade. His robe was black, as was his cloak, both loosely woven from coarse sheep wool, the attire worn by most Jewish merchants. His face was purposely left dirty, an attempt to deepen his fair skin tone to the olive tones of the Jews.

Two things he couldn't hide: his nose and his eyes. His

nose was Roman, not Jewish, and while those from far away countries like Aquitania or Hispania might not be able to detect a difference, to those in Jerusalem, it was instantly obvious. But it was his eyes that set him apart. Rather than the deep brown or black common through most of Judea, his eyes were green, deep green.

The man stood in the shadows as far away from the gate of the palatial home as he could, but still close enough to watch those who entered. He wasn't trying to hide as much as he was simply trying to avoid calling attention to himself. Anyone passing on the street might wonder who he was, but no one would make the effort to question what appeared to be a modestly successful Jew.

He had been standing in the shadows at various places on the street since just after the sun had sunk behind the hills. When no one had entered or left the mansion after two hours, he had begun to think he had been misinformed about the day or location, or perhaps both. He thought of the squirrelly little informant who had told him of the meeting—Jews could be so untrustworthy at times.

Suddenly, from the darkness, a man appeared. He walked up the street briskly and with anxious intent, looking mostly at the ground but tossing an occasional glance over his shoulder. And then another materialized behind him, this one walking much faster. The two arrived at the gate at the same time and greeted each other. The servant who normally stood guard was gone, given the night off by his master, so they pushed the heavy gate open and walked in. The gate had hardly slammed shut when two more men appeared, walking side by side. They too pushed open the gate and entered the compound.

The man watched silently from the shadows as others slowly arrived—twenty-three all together—and made a mental note of the shrill creak the gate made each time it opened and closed. He waited for thirty minutes after the last man arrived.

Then, satisfied no others were coming, he emerged from the shadows and brazenly walked up to the gate. Unlike the others, he cautiously lifted the latch, careful not to make a sound. Then, ever so guardedly, he pushed against the gate, moving it slowly so the hinges wouldn't let out the creaks he'd heard as the other men had passed through. Once inside, he silently closed the gate and crept across the spacious courtyard to a trellis that ran up the side of the house to the roof of a porch. It was an easy climb, and he noiselessly stepped from the trellis to the porch's roof.

Earlier in the day, when he had examined the mansion from outside the high wall, he'd decided that the tile roof would be the biggest problem he would encounter. There was enough pitch to the roof that walking would be difficult, and if any of the tiles were loose, he was sure to slip. If that happened, there would be no stopping until he hit the ground. Whether he survived the fall or not didn't matter. If the fall didn't kill him, the men inside the house would most certainly see to his death. The man shuddered; it was an unpleasant thought, so he pushed it from his mind.

In the daylight, he had estimated the distance from the trellis to the small porch window to be about twenty-five feet. If his information was correct, and he assumed it was because he had blackmailed one of the priests who would be in attendance to get it, that porch window was in the room where the group would be meeting.

He had extracted the information from the priest fairly easily. A few days earlier, he had discovered some unflattering information about the priest's activities and had simply threatened him with exposure if he didn't cooperate. Out of fear of losing his position in the Sanhedrin, the priest more than cooperated. He not only told the man where in the mansion the meeting would be held but suggested that by crouching below the window, he could hear every word that was said. He even volunteered to open the window on condition he never see or hear from the man again. The pretend Jew had agreed to this condition, knowing full well that he never intended to keep his word. He would blackmail the priest again and again if he needed more information.

Crouching low and moving slowly, the man tested the stability of each tile with his toe before trusting his entire weight to it. Only once did he almost slip, and that was due to his own clumsiness rather than a loose tile. After reaching the window, he assumed the only position he could that would allow him to hear without being detected: he squatted down on his legs, his back to the wall. This was going to be a long and uncomfortable night, he told himself as he adjusted his legs to keep them from cramping. The priest had been right; with the window open, he had no trouble hearing every word.

"Simeon," Caiaphas barked, "you're dozing again." The agitation in the high priest's voice was evident to everyone huddled in the room.

"Forgive me," Simeon said meekly. "It has been a very long week of long days and even longer nights."

Caiaphas replied with only slightly less agitation, "They've been long for all of us, and this night will only get longer if you keep dozing off. Tell us what you've learned from your . . . associates." The better word would have been spies, but it didn't matter. All twenty-four men in the room knew exactly what or whom he meant.

"Jesus's popularity is amassing at an alarming rate," Simeon began. "But so are his detractors," he added with a wry smile. "Our efforts to create hostility toward him seem to be working. As we approach Passover, I'm told that several of his closest followers—apostles, he calls them—have warned him against coming to Jerusalem to celebrate the feast. They are concerned there is so much discord that they believe it is unsafe for him."

"Good," Caiaphas interjected. "What else?"

"I'm told an interesting phenomenon is occurring among his followers," Simeon said, leaning back in his chair and rubbing his bloodshot eyes. "It seems that while many people flock to him daily, almost as many leave."

"Really?" Caiaphas said, leaning forward in his chair, his curiosity genuinely piqued.

"They are attracted by the miraculous things he does," Simeon said, looking around the poorly lit room. "We have several reports that he has healed countless people, and on at least two occasions, he has fed thousands of people with nothing more than a few fish and loaves of bread. But the miracles are apparently not enough. The people require a constant show of his power or they seem to lose interest and return to their former ways."

"Interesting," Caiaphas said. "And what of our efforts to portray him as weak rather than the long-awaited military Messiah who will free us from these wretched Romans. Is that having an effect?"

"More than we could have hoped," Simeon replied. "That was a stroke of genius on your part."

"How so?" Caiaphas asked with a measure of satisfaction in his voice.

"When the people listen to his sermons of love rather than war, they argue among themselves about his claim of being the Messiah," Simeon said, shifting his ponderous frame in the uncomfortably small chair. "They want freedom from the oppression of the Romans, and this man proclaims a gospel of love. I have planted a few of our loyal men in the crowds to heckle him on that point whenever they get the chance."

Caiaphas nodded his head in approval as he considered this information. Lifting a small silver cup from the table beside him, he raised it to his lips and sipped sparingly. A devious smile formed on his mouth as he set the cup down. "What about his apostles?" he asked in an almost sinister tone. "Can any of them be persuaded to be more . . . helpful . . . to us?"

"You mean, can they be bribed?" Simeon asked. He shook his head. "These men are devoted to him. I don't think it's likely."

"Well," intoned a deep voice from the shadows on the far side of the room, "there may be one."

Every head in the room turned toward Jahoram, a tall skinny man with sleek, black hair and a sparse but manicured black beard. Unlike the others who lounged around the room in chairs, he stood with his back resting against the wall and his arms folded across his chest.

Caiaphas looked intently at the man and asked, "Who might that be, Jehoram, and why do you think it possible?"

"His name is Judas, the son of Simon from Kerioth. He handles all the money for Jesus and his followers," Jehoram said evenly.

"Can he be . . . persuaded or coerced into helping us?" Caiaphas asked matter-of-factly, as if bribery was an everyday event.

"Perhaps," Jerhoram said cautiously. "I've known him for years. He is an oddity. He can be forceful and strong, but he is also a man of weak character, one whose values seem to shift as circumstances demand."

"What else do you know of his personal life?" Caiaphas probed.

"Not a lot," Jehoram said. "Only that he has debts he never seems able to pay, including one to my family."

Caiaphas leaned toward Jehoram and raised his eyebrows. "How much?" he pressed.

"Thirty pieces of silver," Jehoram answered evenly.

Caiaphas's mind whirled at full speed. "See what you can do," he said to Jerhoram. "And keep me personally informed of the progress you make."

Jehoram nodded his head. "I'll contact him tomorrow."

Turning back to Simeon, Caiaphas asked, "Do we have enough evidence to bring Jesus to trial?"

"No," Simeon responded in a tired voice.

"Not on any charge?" Caiaphas said, looking around the room at the men. "Certainly there must be something: blasphemy, sedition, anything! What about some charge involving the Romans?"

A distinctive-looking man dressed in a flowing gray robe and ornate purple and gold headscarf cleared his throat and said in a low but authoritative voice, "There may be a way."

People who had been looking at Jehoram or Caiaphas now turned their attention to Annas, the oldest and undoubtedly most influential member of the Sanhedrin, and Caiaphas's father-in-law. Years before, the old man had held Caiaphas's position as high priest, but the Romans removed him from the office when they discovered he was plotting a rebellion. The fact that the Romans didn't execute him on the spot attested to his power and influence in the Jewish world. The man was diabolical, treacherous, and a master of manipulating Jewish law to get what he wanted.

"It would be somewhat complicated, but not impossible," Annas said.

A thin smile spread across Caiaphas' lips, and he nodded toward the man. "Please, enlighten us," Caiaphas respectfully said.

The old man shifted his slight body in his chair and leaned forward. "It would involve finding, shall we say, exactly the 'right' witnesses. Men who could be gently guided in their thinking and in the responses they provide the Sanhedrin."

The sleepiness that had hounded Simeon for the past two hours evaporated as Annas cautiously outlined his plan for the entrapment and trial of Jesus.

The group listened quietly for the first fifteen minutes of the scheme. Once Annas had plotted the skeleton of the plan, each man began hanging bits and pieces of flesh on the bones and less than two hours later, they had formulated a plan—a bold plan. It was illegal from start to finish but a bold plan nonetheless—a plan that would ensure the condemnation of Jesus, and, they hoped, his death.

"Excellent," Caiaphas said as he pushed himself to his feet. "It has been a long night but very productive."

Taking their cue from Caiaphas, each of the men quickly rose from his chair, anxious for the comfort of his own home and bed.

The man perched on the tile roof listened as the men rapidly filed from the room. He then sat motionless as he watched them walk out the gate and down the street. Only after all of them had disappeared from sight did he carefully retrace his steps off the roof, across the courtyard, and through the gate, noiselessly fading away into the night.

EIGHT

❋ ❋ ❋ ❋ ❋

"Enter," the Roman centurion commanded in a voice that was accustomed to issuing orders. As he waited for the door to open, he unbuckled the decorative brass clasp of his wide leather belt and removed it, the scabbard, and sword from around his hips. He gently laid the tools of his trade on the table in front of him and rubbed his hip. Even after all these years, or perhaps because of them, it was still a sense of relief to remove the sword from his side.

The door opened and a man dressed in a black robe and cloak with scraggly beard and green eyes entered the nicely appointed room.

"Ah, Justinian," the centurion said with little surprise. "I've been expecting you. What news have you brought me?"

"Long live Caesar," Justinian said as he clapped his right fist to his chest and gingerly walked across the floor. It was a half-hearted utterance, hardly worthy of a member of the Roman legion, but it had been a long night, and it was all the enthusiasm he could muster. The centurion didn't bother to return the salute. He was the man's superior and as such was under no obligation to do so. Besides, one look at the man made it obvious formalities were uncalled for. "You're not walking so well," he said and pointed to a couch made of soft goatskin. "Have a seat."

Justinian grimaced as he hobbled to the inviting piece of furniture with its stack of plush pillows. "I'm happy to be walking at all," he said through a thin smile. The walk from Caiaphas's mansion to the fortress had been slow and painful and did little to salve his aching muscles. With each step, his legs reminded him of the cramped position he had been in, listening to members of the Sanhedrin make their plans to silence Jesus.

The centurion raised his eyebrows inquisitively but said nothing. After many such meetings, he knew Justinian would provide the details of his activities when he was ready. He would never tell everything, unless of course the centurion pressed for details—which he rarely did—but Justinian would say enough. That suited the centurion because he wasn't interested in how or where this man obtained information, only in the information itself.

"How about something to drink?" the centurion asked as he walked to a chair across from Justinian. "Perhaps that will ease your discomfort."

Justinian shook his head. "I'm in greater need of sleep than drink," he replied.

The centurion shrugged his shoulders. "Suit yourself," he said as he picked up a goblet that was resting on the table and, taking a large swallow, lowered himself into a chair.

Two things motivated Justinian to make his report as quick and concise as possible. First, he had spent a long uncomfortable night squatting down and clinging to the tiles of a roof and he was tired. Second, he wanted to soak his legs in warm water and rub ointment on them in an effort to quell the rebellion his muscles were beginning to stage. "You can tell his Excellency he has nothing to worry about from Caiaphas and the Sanhedrin," he said, stretching his legs out in front of him and rubbing his thighs and hamstrings.

The centurion eyed Justinian carefully. "Nothing?" Justinian wasn't sure if it was skepticism or disappointment he detected in the centurion. Looking around the room and all its fine furnishings, he thought it was probably disappointment. This was the lair of a warrior, someone who was accustomed to bloodshed. Several beautifully woven tapestries hung on the walls, the largest of which depicted a battle scene with two men. One was kneeling, his face pressed against the ground. The second man, obviously the conqueror, stood with his foot on the back of the prostrate man's neck. The figure held a spear high in the air, ready to drive it into the man's back. Hanging on other walls around the room was an impressive assortment of swords, spears, and bows—relics of past battles in which the centurion had participated. The entire room suggested war and battles.

"Does that disappoint you?" Justinian asked. "That they aren't planning an uprising?"

"The Jews cause too much trouble. I don't like it, and neither does Pilate," the centurion replied flatly before taking a swallow of liquid. Casually eyeing the goblet in his hand, he asked, "But tell me, what makes you believe we do not have anything to worry about?"

Justinian stopped massaging his legs. "There was no talk of riot or sedition; they aren't planning to overthrow the government."

"Then what did they talk about?"

Justinian moved his legs back and forth in his ongoing effort to ease the stiffness. He didn't even bother to look at the centurion when he said, "They are scheming a way to silence a man from Nazareth, a man named Jesus."

The centurion had been listening carefully before, but at the mention of this name, he sat upright in this chair and placed the goblet on the table. "I know this man," he said in surprise.

Justinian could not hide his own surprise at hearing this. He had known Lucretius Cato for years and had always found him different than the other soldiers he knew. Strong and fearless, he was also a man of compassion and great faith, an odd combination from a Roman centurion. Recovering slightly from the surprise, he asked, "You know him?"

"Yes. I met him—once. It was more than a year ago."

Justinian looked at the Centurion, expecting him to say more, to give some explanation of how he would know about a man from an obscure village miles away from Jerusalem. But an explanation didn't come. Instead, a question: "Why would the Sanhedrin care about silencing this Nazarene?"

"He's a threat to them," Justinian responded, still curious but unwilling to pry.

"The man preaches love and peace! How can that be a threat?"

Justinian raised his eyebrows. "You know what the man teaches?"

It was a baited question, and the centurion immediately picked up on it. Waving his hand as if to dismiss the issue, he said, "Pilate was concerned about Jesus's popularity. We've had people listen to his sermons." It was a nice answer, but Justinian had the impression the centurion wasn't entirely forthcoming.

The centurion looked at Justinian and was about to say something but abruptly changed his mind. Rising to his feet, he stepped in front of Justinian and extended his hand. "You look tired. Go and get some rest—you deserve it. You've done well, Justinian."

The centurion helped Justinian walk across the floor to the door. Reaching for the latch, he said, "You're right, you know."

"About what?" Justinian asked.

NINE

❋ ❋ ❋ ❋ ❋

In the twenty-three years that Joseph had been a member of the Sanhedrin, this was the first time he could recall all seventy-one members being present for a meeting. It simply didn't happen. Illness, business, travel, family matters, and a multitude of other issues always meant at least six and most often ten or twelve members were absent. Joseph mused to himself that some serious threats and arm-twisting must have occurred to make this perfect attendance possible, and he knew that only Caiaphas and his conniving father-in-law, Annas, could exert that kind of influence. Joseph knew whenever an issue was important to them, they would stop at little to get what they wanted, and they wanted Jesus of Nazareth stopped—permanently.

Joseph entered the temple and walked down the corridor to the Chamber of Hewn Stones, the massive hall in which the council met, and wound his way around the large semi-circle of sixty-nine red, overstuffed chairs and their accompanying tables. Two chairs and tables, more ornate than the others, sat perched on a raised platform at the front of the hall. One was for Caiaphas and the other for Simeon. From there they could preside in their official roles as chief high priest and vice chief justice. All in all, there were seventy-one chairs, the exact number prescribed by Jewish law. The large semi-circle in which they were arranged allowed each occupant an unobstructed view of Caiaphas and Simeon as well as every other member of the Sanhedrin. Each could see and be seen without any difficulty as there were no columns, pillars, or dividers to obstruct the view.

Each member had his assigned chair, and as Joseph walked to his, he passed several small clusters of Pharisees and even smaller clusters of Sadducees. These were the men of the Sanhedrin, the supreme judicial tribunal of the Jews.

Dressed in finely woven robes of varying shades of blue, white, brown, and black, and adorned with costly rings and wrist bracelets, they carried on their conversations in hushed tones, often with hands covering their mouths to make it impossible for anyone to read their lips. As Joseph passed each group some men would nod their heads, but none attempted to speak with him. From the looks on their faces, it was obvious to Joseph that the conversations were serious, bordering on ominous. The atmosphere in the room was never lighthearted or jovial, but on this day, the tension was especially thick and oppressive. The hushed tones and subversive glances caused uneasiness in Joseph.

Arriving at his assigned seat, Joseph gathered his robes about him and unceremoniously plopped down. The cushions on the chair were welcome relief for his tired legs, and he let out a long sigh as he settled himself. The table at his right side was empty except for a small goblet filled to the brim with water. Raising the goblet to his mouth, he drank deeply of the cool water. As soon as he set the goblet down, a young man materialized from out of nowhere and replenished it.

"Thank you," Joseph said with a sincere smile.

The boy said nothing but gave a slight bow and then disappeared as quickly as he had appeared, eager to avoid calling any attention to himself.

Joseph stretched out his legs, crossing them at the ankles. His feet ached from a morning of rapid walking from his house to his place of business and now to the temple, and he wished he could soak them in a tub of warm water, even if only for a few minutes. At the very least, he wanted to take off his sandals and rub some oil on his feet with his hands. But he knew neither could happen, so he contented himself with rubbing his feet together as he slowly gazed around the well-appointed hall.

Thick purple drapes had been pulled back from the windows, which allowed ample light to stream in and soften the coldness of the high marble and masonry block walls. The sunlight also allowed him to clearly see each of the men as they sat in their seats or stood in groups. He knew them all. Not in a personal sense, for only a few of them could be considered close friends, but he had spent countless hours in this hall with these men, and he knew where each stood on matters of God and Jewish doctrine.

By and large, they were good men with an almost bottomless depth of knowledge of Jewish law and doctrine. They were considered sages, wise men who could distinguish truth from falsehood and who could be trusted to impose sentences with compassion and fairness. Indeed, the rules of the Sanhedrin required each of them to be married and the father of children, for, they reasoned, only a father could be sufficiently merciful to pass judgment on wayward people.

Only the most serious matters ever made it to this group, matters that were often life and death such as adultery, murder, and blasphemy. Anything of lesser concern was settled by lower courts. The Sanhedrin had the power to pass a death sentence if the crime warranted it, but since the Romans had conquered Jerusalem, they could not execute anyone without Roman sanction. That galled most of them because they hated Roman rule, but long ago Caiaphas had distinguished himself as someone who could expertly finesse a situation in which a death sentence could be carried out without raising the ire or awareness of the Romans. That ability, coupled with his marriage to the former high priest's daughter, enabled him to rise to a leadership position in the Sanhedrin.

A hush fell over the room as a side door to the chamber opened. Caiaphas and Simeon strode into the room arrayed in their priestly robes. Every man abruptly stopped talking and quickly moved to his assigned seat. As if on command, anyone who was sitting rose to their feet so that by the time the two men reached their seats on the raised platform, everyone was quietly standing in front of their assigned chair.

Joseph pushed himself from the comfort of his chair and stood on his aching feet. It was respect for the office the two men held, not the men themselves, which caused him and the other sixty-eight men to stand quietly. Joseph knew there were many members who believed as he did—that Caiaphas was little more than a conniving and scheming power-seeker bent on securing a long lasting place for himself and his family in the ruling society of Judah, but he also knew Caiaphas had a strong power base of loyal supporters.

"Greetings, my brethren," Caiaphas called out and motioned for them all to be seated. The quiet in the room was replaced with the rustle of robes and squeaking of chairs as seventy men lowered themselves; only Caiaphas remained standing.

"There is only one matter before the Sanhedrin this day," Caiaphas said in a booming voice that filled every corner of the hall, "and that is to hear discussion concerning Jesus of Nazareth." He paused, as if to let the words sink in, and then added in a much stronger and louder voice, "A known dissenter and blasphemer."

His words touched off a low rumble of voices that swept through the room as members leaned over to confer with the person sitting beside them or make hushed comments to nobody in particular. It was unheard of for the high priest to level a charge against someone, especially since the accused wasn't even present. The law dictated that the Sanhedrin was to be an impartial tribunal, yet with his initial statement, Caiaphas had tainted the discussion. It was a blatant attempt to prejudice the outcome.

Joseph looked around the room. Some heads bobbed in agreement while others shook from side to side in dismay at Caiaphas's brazen statement. Joseph watched as annoyance, indifference, curiosity, and other emotions spread across the faces of most of his brethren. Regardless of the emotion, nobody questioned that Caiaphas was going to use this meeting to sway opinion and create support for his effort to find a solution to the thorny problem of Jesus of Nazareth.

Gideon, an expert in the law, was the first to jump to his feet. "Honorable Caiaphas," he bellowed in a deep baritone voice, "certainly we all agree that this Nazarene deserves the attention of this council, for only a deaf man could not have heard of his teachings and claims, but no charges have been brought against him. Yet your statement reads as one not only accused but also found guilty."

"Agreed!" shouted a voice from across the room. In quick succession, ten or twelve other voices sounded from other places in the hall, each echoing the same sentiment, and Joseph could see a dozen more men silently nodding their heads in agreement.

Caiaphas took a deep breath and raised his hands in an effort to squelch the rebuttal so he could speak. Without addressing Gideon's main objection, he said, "Gideon makes an excellent point when he says only the deaf are unaware of his teachings, which is precisely why we are obligated," he paused for effect, "yes, *obligated* to investigate this blasphemer and bring him to justice."

Caiaphas' words ignited a rush of emotion, and the room

again erupted in a flurry of voices. If his initial statement hadn't caused division and emotion, his last one most certainly did. Caiaphas gazed around the room and did nothing to stop the clamor. Joseph looked intently at Caiaphas in disbelief at this breach of Sanhedrin protocol. Then he saw the sly smile that quickly appeared and disappeared from Caiaphas's face. Joseph ground his teeth together. This was exactly what the man wanted; Caiaphas was purposely exciting emotion. He was attempting to divide the Sanhedrin.

Almost immediately, six men jumped to their feet, including Diblaim, the man in the chair next to Joseph. Each shouted in unison, "We agree with Caiaphas. Whether charged or not, Jesus is guilty of blasphemy, and we should bring him to trial."

Joseph turned to face the man as he sat down. "Since when does the Sanhedrin bring men to trial? You're perverting the law, Diblaim. We listen when cases are brought to us, but our laws forbid us from seeking out people and bringing them to trial."

"There are times, Joseph, when the welfare of the people supersedes our law, and this is one of those times. This man must be stopped." The words rolled effortlessly off Diblaim's tongue, and Joseph instantly knew it was a rehearsed response that Caiaphas or someone close to him had coached Diblaim and others to say.

On the far side of the room, one of the oldest members rose on unsteady legs and supported himself with a cane in each hand. The man's flowing beard and snowy white hair attested to his age and gave him a look of credibility. Jacobeth of Bethlehem had served in the Sanhedrin longer than anyone, and that alone commanded respect. The room fell silent.

"Brethren, I beg your attention," he began in a shaky voice, not much louder than a whisper. "For reasons I don't understand and do not endorse, Caiaphas has this day chosen to level charges against a man I have known since he was a child. I propose that we discontinue any discussion on the matter and approach this in accordance with our law."

Shouts of "Agreed!" filled the hall. But louder voices shouted, "Let us discuss this Jesus of Nazareth here and now!"

Caiaphas raised his hands in the air and yelled over the roar, "Brethren, quiet! We must have order!" Gradually the talking subsided and semi-quiet returned to the hall. "I am fully aware of my unprecedented statement. But we are in perilous times, which demand dramatic action. What say we vote on the matter? If the majority of the Sanhedrin votes in favor of proceeding, we will do so. If the majority opposes the discussion, we will adjourn."

Joseph looked at Caiaphas with scorn. This was Caiaphas at his best. He was certain that Caiaphas would have enough votes to proceed or he would never have suggested it. Joseph was helpless to stop it. Suddenly things were becoming much clearer. Now he understood why there was perfect attendance, and it also explained why Simeon had been at the old man's house so late the other night and probably many other nights as well. They had been planning and scheming for weeks; of that Joseph was certain.

"All those wishing to proceed with a discussion of Jesus of Nazareth, shout out!" The roar of shouts that filled the hall was almost deafening.

"Those opposed, make it known," Caiaphas said, and Joseph joined his loud cry with a score of other men to voice their disapproval.

The shouts for and against were too similar in volume to determine a clear majority, and a look of surprise spread over Caiaphas's face. He hadn't expected this. He had staged this in an attempt to demonstrate to those opposed to him that he had a clear mandate from the overwhelming majority of the Sanhedrin to freely persecute and prosecute Jesus. But suddenly it was too close to call, and he turned to Simeon for guidance. The two men conferred briefly before Caiaphas again faced the semi-circle of men and said, "The voting is too close to distinguish a course of action by voice alone. We shall vote by a show of hands."

It was impossible not to notice several members as they squirmed in their seats, uncomfortable with Caiaphas' announcement. A voice count had allowed them to shout their preference as part of a group, making it difficult for anyone to later identify exactly how they had voted. Now, they were being forced to publicly declare their position on Jesus of Nazareth.

"All those in favor of proceeding with a discussion of Jesus of Nazareth raise your hand high," Caiaphas shouted.

Joseph quickly scanned the room as hands went into the air. Some shot up without hesitation, but more, far more, were raised slowly, hesitantly. *This would be close*, he thought as he counted. One, two . . . ten, eleven . . . twenty-three, twenty-four, and then thirty. He had only a few more hands to count when Simeon bellowed triumphantly, "Thirty-eight!"

That was it—the majority, but a very slender one. Caiaphas wasted no time initiating the discussion with a vitriolic recounting of statements Jesus made about his divine Sonship. Using half-truths and taking comments out of context, his tone and words were carefully chosen to incense the non-committed members, and it was working. As soon as Caiaphas concluded his opening remarks, others immediately jumped in with equally inflammatory statements.

For the next ninety minutes, Caiaphas orchestrated a succession of accusations, recognizing only those men Joseph was certain had been handpicked and groomed in exactly what to say. Finally, after shouts of complaint from a number of other members, he recognized three members opposed to the discussion and entire proceedings. Their voices were drowned out with occasional heckling and booing from those members who supported Caiaphas.

The entire proceeding was a farce. Caiaphas only barely managed to keep things under control. Tempers rose and outbursts were common. Never had Joseph seen such a disgusting display of impropriety and disregard for common courtesy as he was now witnessing. And more disturbing was Caiaphas's complete unwillingness to stop the uproar among members of the Sanhedrin. In fact, there were times when he encouraged it.

Joseph folded his arms across his chest and looked across the room at Gamaliel, a doctor of the law, a Pharaisee, a man held in high honor among the people, and one of the most respected members of the Sanhedrin. The man sat stoically observing the debacle. He had stirred in his seat a time or two and even made one attempt to rise to his feet to speak, but he had been outmaneuvered by others who were quicker and more vocal. Finally, the distinguished man found an opening and took advantage of it. Rising, he boomed out, "My brethren, peace be unto you! We are behaving not as learned men but as rabid dogs attacking an injured rabbit." The rebuke was sharp and had the desired effect, for the chattering quickly died and silence prevailed.

With order restored, Gamaliel said powerfully, "You men of Israel, consider carefully what you intend to do with this man Jesus. Do you not remember some time ago that Theudas appeared among us claiming to be an important somebody, and about four hundred people rallied around him? He was killed, and all his followers scattered."

After pausing long enough to let the statement settle in their minds, he continued. "After him, Jonas the Galilean appeared in the days of the census and led a band of people in revolt. He too was killed, and all his followers were scattered. Therefore, in this matter of Jesus, I advise you to leave the man alone. Let him be! If his purpose and activity is of human origin, it will fail. But if it is of God, you will not be able to stop him or his followers." Then, looking directly at

Caiaphas, he concluded, "And you will only find yourselves fighting against God." Turning slightly to make sure he was aligned with his chair, he lowered himself down, reached for his goblet of water, and took a drink.

The effect was startling. Every eye was riveted on him. No one said a word or stirred. At that moment, Joseph rose to his feet, his robes falling silently around him. Swallowing hard and taking a deep breath, he stood motionless until he was certain that everyone had shifted his attention to him.

"Brethren, I have sat these past two hours observing and listening as charges and countercharges have been hurled back and forth. Never in my years in the Sanhedrin have I witnessed so great a division amongst us." Looking directly at Caiaphas, he continued, "Our distinguished leader has this day done an admirable job of inciting this division, the ultimate purpose for which he alone knows."

Pausing to look into the faces of the men in the room, Joseph said with even greater emphasis, "On three occasions, I have met with this Jesus. Not as part of a large group, but in a small house in the lower city with only a few of his closest associates and friends." Looking around the room, he could see the shock in the faces of many of his fellow members of the Sanhedrin, but he pressed on. "I have had the opportunity to ask questions, to hear answers, and have of myself reached a conclusion about him." Turning once again to face Caiaphas, he said in an even, steady voice, "I believe he is the Son of God, the promised Messiah for whom we have prayed and waited for so long."

The silence was deafening. Not a single man stirred in his seat; there was no clanking of goblets on tables or shuffling of robes. Seventy pairs of eyes looked at Joseph, some in disbelief, others in anger, and a few in pity, but most simply looked on without emotion.

"I agree with my learned friend Gamaliel; we should allow

this Jesus to have his freedom," Joseph continued. "Attempting to bring him to trial and sentencing him, even if to death, will not silence his teachings or end his fame, because unlike Theudas or Jonas of Galilee, this man is from God."

Joseph stopped speaking and looked once more at Caiaphas. As their eyes locked in an intense stare, Joseph watched words form on Caiaphas's lips: "I will destroy you!"

Without acknowledging the threatening words, Joseph turned and slowly walked toward the door that would lead him from the hall. The only noise in the room was the muted sound of his sandals as he walked across the tiled floor. Only as he approached Nicodemus did he slow his pace long enough to look into the man's eyes. For the briefest of moments, Nicodemus held his gaze, and it seemed to Joseph as if he might stand and say something, but the thought had no sooner entered his head than Nicodemus broke eye contact and looked at the floor. *So that's how it is to be*, he thought. Not even his friend Nicodemus was willing to stand with him and come to the defense of Jesus. *No matter*, he thought and strode toward the door. Joseph had spoken his conviction, knowing full well that his words would result in expulsion from the Sanhedrin and possibly his financial ruin.

Ten

A h, my dear Devorah, it's so kind of you to come see your old cousin," Caiaphas said as he rose from his chair and walked toward her. "Please, can I get you something cool to drink, or perhaps a piece of dried fruit and some nuts?" he asked as he gave her a small hug.

"Thank you, but no, I'm quite satisfied," Devorah said, kissing him lightly on his cheek.

"The weather has been delightful this spring, hasn't it?" Caiaphas said as he gently guided her toward a chair.

Devorah smiled slightly. "Indeed."

The pleasant little exchange caught Devorah slightly off guard. It was not like her forceful cousin to make small talk. Although he was always pleasant, since their childhood, he had been far more inclined to abruptness when talking with her. He was never rude, but always to the point. In fact, this entire meeting was out of character for him. She had been curiously suspicious about the meeting ever since Caiaphas's servant had delivered a message earlier that morning, requesting that she come to his home. Always in the past, when he wanted to speak with her, he stopped at her house or they talked at social gatherings. She couldn't recall a single occasion when he had asked her to come to his home for anything other than dinner or some social function.

"You're undoubtedly wondering why I asked you to come to my home," Caiaphas said as he waved off a servant who had appeared to see if anything was needed.

Devorah smiled at the directness of the statement. This was the Caiaphas she knew. But as much as she liked the man, she felt the need to be guarded in her response, so she said, "Yes, the thought has crossed my mind."

"Devorah, you know me as well as anyone," he began.

The statement had no truth to it, of course, because over the years, Caiaphas had carefully developed two sides of his life. There was the outwardly considerate man, the man who smiled at the people, hugged little children, and kissed old poverty-stricken widows while expressing dismay at their destitute situation. That was the man Devorah knew, the public man, the man whom the people genuinely respected. But then there was the other man, the man Devorah had no idea existed, the man who was manipulative, deceitful, and quite capable of planning insurrection and death if it suited him. "You know me well," Caiaphas repeated. "And that's why this conversation is so difficult for me." It was another lie. There was nothing difficult about this conversation. He had carefully rehearsed it and was confident he knew exactly how it would go.

Devorah said nothing as she folded her hands in her lap and forced a smile.

"How are things with Joseph, er, I mean, between you and Joseph? Are they well?"

Cousin or not, the question was too direct for Devorah, and she fidgeted in her seat. "What are you asking, Caiaphas?" she answered warily.

He looked directly at her, squeezed his lips tightly together, and furrowed his brow, giving the appearance of serious and grave concern. He waited, as if contemplating how to proceed, but the pause was for effect, not a search for the right words.

"I'm worried about you," he said with feigned concern, "or perhaps more correctly, I'm worried about Joseph."

"And why is that?" she replied.

Another pause, this one longer. "I am deeply troubled by his actions," he said slowly and gravely.

"What actions?" Devorah asked, tipping her head slightly in a quizzical pose.

Caiaphas abandoned his efforts to be discreet and attacked the issue head on: "How much time has he been spending with this Jesus of Nazareth?"

Devorah breathed the slightest of gasps at the question, but as barely noticeable as it was, it spoke volumes to Caiaphas—he had hit a nerve.

Devorah said nothing. She unfolded her hands and almost immediately folded them again. She looked directly at Caiaphas, churning over in her mind exactly what she was going to say. Scrunching the small silk cloth she held in her hands, she meekly said, "Cousin, I need your help and advice."

The words were like music to Caiaphas, and he leaned forward, lightly patting Devorah's knee in a kindly gesture of reassurance. The outward look of concern on his face perfectly veiled the inward smile. She was hooked. All he had to do was play her just right, and he would shove Joseph one step further to destruction. Joseph of Arimathea was about to lose his position in the Sanhedrin, his membership in the synagogue, and if he did this correctly, his wife would divorce him. All for this pretender who dared to proclaim himself the Son of God. Caiaphas would not only eliminate the threat of Jesus, he would destroy those who supported him as well.

"Devorah," he said reassuringly, "you know I'll help you however I can, but to do that I'll need to know what Joseph's involvement has been with Jesus."

For reasons unknown to him, Caiaphas always found it a little unnerving watching a woman cry, and he found it especially so now as the tears streamed down his cousin's face. When she regained her composure, Devorah said, "I'm sorry. I don't mean to cry, but this situation has been stressful."

"It's quite all right, Devorah. I understand," he said with as much feigned sympathy as he could muster.

"I really don't know the first time Joseph went to talk with Jesus," she said. "It could have been months or even a year ago. The first that I became aware of it was just a few months ago. He came home late one night, or more accurately, very early in the morning after having been out all night." Devorah paused to take a deep breath. "When I questioned him about where he'd been, he was evasive. He said he had been out discussing religion. I assumed he had been out with members of the Sanhedrin and thought nothing more of it, but several nights later, he was out late again."

Caiaphas shifted his weight in the chair and leaned forward, resting his elbows on his knees. "So you rightfully asked him again, I assume."

"Yes. Only then I was much more direct. At first he offered the same explanation, but when I pressed him, he finally admitted he had been meeting with Jesus. I was devastated, Caiaphas, because I've heard much about this Jesus, and not all of it is good. We ended up in a rather heated argument."

"I see," Caiaphas said, leaning back in his chair.

Before he could say anything more, Devorah continued, "I've avoided having anything to do with Jesus or even discussing him with the other women, which has been difficult. Surely you know how virtually everyone speaks of him."

"Indeed I do," Caiaphas said, nodding his head.

"I explained to Joseph that this Jesus could have serious consequences for him and for me. I told him by associating with the man that our very livelihood and position in the community was at stake," she said, her voice getting stronger and filling with emotion. "I really thought that would be the end of it because he readily agreed with me."

"But it hasn't ended there, has it?" Caiaphas prompted.

Devorah looked her cousin in the eye and in a soft voice said, "No, it hasn't. Just this week, he once again came home from another meeting late at night. We had another argument, not as long or serious, but still we exchanged words, and I told him he must choose between me and this Jesus."

At that remark, Caiaphas sat upright in his chair. Trying to camouflage his enthusiasm, he asked, "You said that? You told him that?"

"I did."

"And what was his response?"

"He hasn't given me a response," Devorah replied with sadness in her voice.

"I see," he said and eased himself slightly backward in his chair. This was going better than he had hoped, and he suppressed the urge to smile. He would teach Joseph and the other members of the Sanhedrin who dared to be disloyal to him that it would cost them dearly.

"Knowing what you have told me, Devorah," Caiaphas said in a hushed tone, "will make what I'm about to tell you difficult. This is very painful for me to say, and it won't be easy for you to hear, but it must be said."

Caiaphas watched as she bit her lower lip. He couldn't help but notice she contined to twist the small cloth she held in her hands.

He began slowly. "Yesterday during a meeting of the Sanhedrin," he paused, suddenly wishing he didn't have to hurt his cousin this way, "Joseph stood before the entire body and publicly announced his support and belief in this Jesus of Nazareth."

A look of shock spread over Devorah's face, and she stopped biting her lip and wringing the cloth. Caiaphas was expecting one of two reactions when he told Devorah about

Joseph's proclamation. Either she would break out in a flood of tears, which he dreaded, or she would be furiously angry, which he hoped. The anger, he was confident, he could channel against Joseph and hasten his downfall. But Devorah did neither. Instead, she sat silently, as motionless as stone, and stared straight ahead at some unseen object in the distance.

Uncertain exactly what to do, Caiaphas did nothing. He sat quietly in his chair watching Devorah. After a few moments, he noticed she again absently twisted the silk cloth in her hands and moved her toes in her sandals. Suddenly, without unnecessary movement, she pushed herself from the chair. Caiaphas rose quickly and stood facing her.

"Thank you, Caiaphas," she said. "Believe it or not, you have helped me." She abruptly turned and walked out of the room without giving him a chance to respond.

ELEVEN

There was no yelling, screaming, or name calling, but there was anger, disappointment, and sorrow.

Joseph paused as he walked across the courtyard of his comfortable estate and examined a deep red rose that was beginning to bloom. It was Devorah's favorite color, and he bent over and inhaled deeply, savoring the sweet fragrance that filled his nose. The aroma caused his mind to flood with memories of happier times, times when the laughter of Devorah and the children filled the air of the courtyard. Smiling at the memory, he straightened up and walked toward a side doorway that entered directly into the kitchen area. He rarely used this entrance, but the acid in his stomach started churning not long after the servant had delivered the message, and he wanted something to calm it down, perhaps a crust of bread or a few dried dates dipped in honey.

As he neared the kitchen door, he again turned over in his mind the unusual nature of the written message Devorah had sent. Many times in the past, Pehulah, one of Devorah's household servants, had been sent with messages to the large storage building that housed Joseph's business, although in the past, it had always been a verbal message, never written. Devorah would tell him exactly what he was to say and then make him repeat it back to her at least four or five times to be certain he had it engrained in his memory. When he arrived at the building, Pehulah would find Joseph and deliver the message, or if Joseph was busy, he would tell it exactly as he rehearsed it to one of Joseph's assistants. After that, he would amble back to the mansion, stopping frequently to gawk at the merchandise of street vendors or chat with pretty servant girls who had been sent on errands by their masters.

Although Joseph didn't know it as he lifted the latch to the kitchen door, this time everything was different. Devorah had called Pehulah out onto the veranda, out of sight and hearing of any other servants, and handed him a small bit of rolled parchment. In a very somber voice, she said, "You are to immediately deliver this to Master Joseph, and only him. Do not give it to anyone but him." Continuing, she said, "Do not stop along the way and talk to the pretty girls as you usually do. Go directly there and return as quickly as you can—no stopping, is that clear?"

"Is that all? Is there no message I am to speak to Master Joseph?" Pehulah asked in surprise as he took the roll and stuffed it inside his tunic. He couldn't help noticing that his mistress avoided eye contact as she spoke, but it was impossible not to see the redness of her eyes and the stress-induced lines in her brow.

"No, nothing further," Devorah said, turning away from him. "Hurry now!"

Pehulah turned and quickly walked from the veranda, once more wishing he knew how to read, for he would love to know what the strange characters on the rolled scrap of parchment said; undoubtedly they would explain the redness in his mistress's eyes.

Pehulah did almost exactly as Devorah instructed. Except for the few brief minutes when he stopped to talk with the beautiful servant girl who served Anna and Nicodemus, he had raced down the streets of Jerusalem to Joseph's large building filled with sacks of grain stacked to the ceiling, row upon row of barrels of olive oil, huge casks of wine, and rooms full of costly and exotic merchandise. He trotted in the door, completely out of breath, only to see Joseph deep in negotiations with a boisterous Greek merchant who was as wide as he was tall. He briefly considered interrupting the discussion to deliver his message but decided against it. He much preferred the easy life of a servant in the big mansion to sweating away in his master's stables, and interrupting the discussion would ensure immediate passage to the stench of manure and shoveling muck from stalls.

Realizing he had no choice but to sit and wait, he plopped down on a small bench outside the main door. His hard seat was mostly out of earshot of the two men, but he could easily watch the little Greek as he spoke, gesturing with his hands with every word and strutting around the room whenever Joseph spoke. At first he had tried to eavesdrop on the conversation, but when he realized they were speaking Greek rather than Aramaic, he gave up. Pehulah spoke only a smattering of Greek, not nearly enough to even guess what they were talking about, so he contented himself with soaking up the pleasant late morning air and springtime sunshine.

Finally, after more than an hour, the short round Greek came bounding out of the door in a huff and brushed past Pehulah. Jumping to his feet, he quickly walked through the door and strode to where Joseph stood. "Excuse me, master, I have a message from the mistress," he said, bowing from the waist.

"What is it, Pehulah?" Joseph said with a smile, expecting the youth to repeat a verbal message from his wife.

Pehulah reached inside his tunic, withdrew the parchment, and handed it to Joseph. He was unsure what to do next. Should he leave or wait? Would he be given a verbal message and sent back to the mansion, or would his master make some of those strange marks on the parchment that Pehulah couldn't decipher? He didn't know what to do. Nothing quite like this had ever happened before. So Pehulah stood still and waited.

Joseph took the small scrap, which was slightly more flexible now, having absorbed some of the heat and moisture from the servant's body. He easily unrolled it and read the words it contained.

Pehulah watched Joseph's eyes as they moved across the paper. They only went back and forth three times before he looked up. He couldn't tell what Joseph was looking at, but he didn't think it was anything—he was just staring blankly, looking across the room into nothingness. Pehulah watched Joseph's chest expand and contract in a deep sigh. His master's eyes again went back and forth across the paper three times.

Joseph slowly lowered his hands to his sides, almost letting the small scrap slip from his fingers to the floor. The normal radiant expression on his face was replaced with a gloomy countenance and distress.

"Thank you, Pehulah, for delivering this. You may now return to the mansion. Please tell my wife I shall be there as quickly as possible."

"Yes, master," Pehulah said, turning and racing for the door, his sense of curiosity at the note's contents now extinguished. He was now far more concerned about the change that had spread over his master's face as he read the note and if its message would affect him and his position in the mansion. As soon as he got home, he would discuss all this with the other servants to see if they had any insight to what it all meant.

Joseph pushed open the door to the kitchen and stepped inside, quietly closing the door behind him. It was a large room with cupboards made of mahogany and olive wood. Clay pots filled with cooking ingredients were neatly arranged on shelves, and a few metal pots hung suspended from the ceiling. It was neat and clean. But for all its orderliness, Joseph had no idea where to look for a morsel of bread to calm his stomach. He never came here for food; it was always brought to him. Spying a bowl filled with dates sitting on an old and ornately carved table off to the side of the room, he walked over to them. He picked one up and plopped it in his mouth, being careful not to crunch down on the pit. Spitting the pit into a small earthen container beside the table, he put another in his mouth.

After eating two, Joseph licked the honey from his thumb and index finger. He debated eating more but had no appetite. The dates were to calm the acid in his stomach not satisfy the gnawing from hunger. If he was hungry after talking with Devorah, he would ask a servant to prepare a more substantial noon-day meal for him; if not, he would return to his business and wait for dinner.

Joseph walked down a long hallway toward a sitting room and called Devorah's name. It was where she spent much of her time when she was pondering things, and he expected to find her there. Arriving at the doorway, he looked inside and gently called her name again. Not seeing her, he turned down another hall, calling her name as he passed several more rooms of the mansion. Leaving the main house, he walked down a breeze-way. There on the veranda that overlooked the city, his wife was sitting at a small table with her hands folded in her lap.

Hearing footfalls in the hallway, Devorah turned her head and watched her husband of forty years approach. She admitted to herself that even though he had slowed and bent slightly with age, he was still an imposing figure.

"Good afternoon, Devorah. I'm sorry I'm late," he said lightheartedly. "Old Constantine stopped and tried to convince me to join him in a scheme of outfitting a ship to some Greek islands to trade olive oil for carpets."

Devorah gave a quick and half-hearted smile. She looked at him with coolness. The impression Joseph had felt as he read her face was instantly confirmed—he knew what was about to follow would not be pleasant.

"Please, Joseph, sit down," she said flatly, motioning to the empty chair across the table from her.

Joseph made no effort to speak; he simply did as she bid without hesitation. As he settled into the chair, he thought how he had never liked the table or the chairs that surrounded it—the legs were too short, and it sat too close to the ground. He'd tried several times to get rid of it, but Devorah wouldn't hear of it. It fit her perfectly, and she loved it.

Joseph was about to comment about the table but then decided against it. Devorah had orchestrated this situation, and he would let her proceed at her own pace. Laying both hands on the table, he interlocked his fingers and sat quietly, waiting for what he knew was coming.

"Joseph," she said, her voice even and measured. "After you left this morning I received a message from Caiaphas inviting me to his home. He wanted to talk."

Joseph looked into her eyes but said nothing.

Devorah shifted slightly in her chair so that she was facing him directly and, in a calm voice, asked, "Is it true? Did you say the things to the Sanhedrin that he said you did?"

Joseph unfolded his hands and leaned back in the chair. "What did the old man tell you I said?" he asked cautiously.

"That you defended Jesus of Nazareth. That you said you believe him to be the Messiah," she replied in a quivering voice. "Is it true? Did you say those things?"

Joseph leaned forward and reached across the table to grasp Devorah's hand, but she recoiled, pulling back out of his reach. "Answer me!" she said sharply.

Withdrawing his hands, Joseph instead folded them on the table and said nothing, watching her dab tears that were forming in the corners of her eyes with a blue and gold colored silk cloth.

Joseph had worried this moment might come. He had hoped and prayed it wouldn't, but deep down he knew it was destined to happen. He rose from his chair and took a few steps to the railing that encircled the veranda. With his back to her, he said, "Yes, it is true."

"You've chosen, then? You've chosen Jesus over me?"

Joseph turned and faced her, "Why must you view it like that? Why do you insist I must choose between you and him?"

"Because you can't have it both ways," she replied. "His ways are not our ways, Joseph. The things he teaches are not of God. Can't you see that?"

"What I see is a man whose every action and word instills in me a desire to be a better person, a man whose teachings and example will lead us, you and me, to a better life."

"No, Joseph. Not a better life. A ruined life," Devorah corrected. "He will ruin our lives and deprive us of everything we have."

"So that's it," Joseph said, returning to the chair. "This isn't about belief in baptism, salvation, redemption, or the promised Messiah. This is about what our belief in those things will cost us," Joseph said as he sat down. Then waving his arms about him, he said with more force than he intended, "This is about a fine home, beautiful clothes, and a place in society, isn't it?"

Devorah was startled by the question but retorted, "It's about what we've been taught; it's about our traditions and our heritage." She said the words without any heartfelt conviction, and both of them knew it.

Joseph leaned back in his chair and looked at his wife for a long moment. "It's about those things for me as well, Devorah, but you must understand it's about me being willing to give them all up for the gospel Jesus teaches." Joseph paused to choke back the rising emotion in his throat. "I would rather go through the rest of my life as a beggar and have the gospel of Jesus than go through it with all our wealth and not have it."

Devorah looked at her husband, trying to discern if he really believed what he had just said. They sat in silence for a long moment before she said, "Will you answer a question for me?"

"Anything you ask," Joseph replied.

"When did you first meet with Jesus?"

Joseph didn't hesitate. "I met him about two years ago while on my way to Sychar in Samaria. It was a casual meeting, purely accidental. I stopped just outside the town at Jacob's well for water, and he was there talking with a woman. It surprised me to see a Jewish man talking to a Samaritan woman, and while I drew water from the well, I listened to their conversation."

Devorah didn't show any emotion. "And?" she asked.

"He told her he could give her living water—water that would quench her thirst forever. The woman thought he spoke of some magical water and eagerly wanted it. Then he explained it was spiritual water, and he was talking about eternal life."

"That's it?"

"Then he asked the woman about her husband, and she replied she didn't have a husband. He told her she had answered correctly. Somehow this stranger knew she had had five different husbands, and the man she now had wasn't her husband. The woman jumped up and proclaimed that he was a prophet because he knew her past, and she hurried off to tell all the people there was a prophet and that they should come listen."

"Did you say anything to him?" Devorah asked inquisitively.

"Yes, of course," Joseph said. "I introduced myself, and I asked him about this doctrine of eternal life and how he knew about the woman's husbands. He answered those questions, but he also gave me answers to questions I have had for a long time. Soon after, some of his followers, his apostles, returned with food to eat, and they invited me to eat with them. As we ate, I listened to them discuss many subjects. Finally, we left, going our different ways."

Devorah looked at Joseph. "Did you meet with him often after that?"

"No, I didn't even encounter him again until just a few months ago. Since then, though, I have met with him and some of his closest followers on several occasions."

Devorah tossed her head to shake the hair from the sides of her face. "It was during these last meetings that you became a believer, then?

"Yes," Joseph said with conviction. "Devorah, you must understand that none of this was done with any intention of hurting you. I was hoping you would come to understand and believe as I do. I do not want this to become a wedge between us."

"Your hopes are in vain, Joseph. It is a wedge," Devorah said without emotion. "I have no interest in Jesus of Nazareth or any of his beliefs. He is trouble. And like others who have come before him, he will win a few people over with his tricks and deceit and then be gone."

The two of them sat looking at each other, neither quite sure what to do next. Finally, Joseph rose from his chair, leaned over, and gently placed his hand on hers. He expected her to recoil at his touch, but she didn't. "I'm sorry, Devorah. I truly love you," he said. Then, withdrawing his hand, he walked from the room.

TWELVE

❖ ❖ ❖ ❖ ❖ ❖ ❖

"How did it go with Devorah?" Simeon asked as Caiaphas sat down at the table.

"Very well! Very well, indeed," Caiaphas replied, looking at the table spread with dishes of roast lamb, dried fruit, bread, and dates. "I'm hungry. Let's give thanks to Jehovah for this food and eat."

Both men bowed their heads while Caiaphas offered a short prayer of thanks. Then they rolled up the sleeves of their robes, dipped their hands in dishes of water, and patted them dry on cloths.

"Their marriage is over," Caiaphas said as he unfolded a small cloth and placed it on his lap.

Simeon smiled as he did the same. "You're certain?" he asked.

"Without question. She was furious when she left my palace this morning," Caiaphas said. "I'm certain that as we sit here and eat, she and Joseph are in the midst of a serious discussion, a discussion that will ultimately end in their divorce and his humiliation."

Simeon nodded his head and was about to say something when Caiaphas continued, "But their divorce is only the first step. There are still other things we must do to ensure Joseph's destruction for his actions, and we must move quickly. It must be done in one all-encompassing stroke." He speared a piece of roasted lamb with the point of his knife and stuck it in his mouth.

Simeon casually glanced around the small room in the temple in which they were eating their mid-day meal and lifted a clay cup to take a drink. "I agree, but we must be cautious and proceed very methodically. Do you have a plan in mind?" he asked.

"Only the basics," Caiaphas replied through a mouthful of meat.

Simeon replaced the cup and wiped his mouth with a small cloth. "It seems to me his excommunication from the synagogue must come first and then his removal from the Sanhedrin. That would be the simplest way."

"I agree," Caiaphas said as he broke a small chunk from a loaf of bread.

"But I see a problem."

"And that is?" Caiaphas asked, popping the bread in his mouth.

"We do not control his membership in the synagogue. We may be priests and members of the Sanhedrin, but we have no control over the synagogues and their councils. Membership is determined by them, not us."

Caiaphas held up his hand, his mouth too full of bread and meat to make an immediate response. After he had chewed and swallowed, he said in the tone of a teacher to a pupil, "My friend, while we may not be able to take part in the formal action, you forget we can exert influence, shall we say, on the decision. Don't forget, Simeon, that I have a very close relationship with Hillel, the ruler of Joseph's synagogue. With a few timely words, I'm confident we can encourage him to see things our way."

Simeon smiled at Caiaphas, but only briefly. "I'm aware of

that, Caiaphas, but it isn't Hillel's willingness to see things our way that is of concern to me. It's the other ten men who sit on the synagogue's council that may not be so easily persuaded. Have you given thought to them?"

Caiaphas took a deep drink of water from his cup. "If we take care of Hillel, the rest will follow."

Simeon gave a lethargic nod of his head; he wasn't quite so confident. "When will you talk with Hillel?"

"Today, as soon as we finish eating," Caiaphas said. "This roast lamb is excellent."

Other than his father-in-law, Annas, there were few men Caiaphas respected as much as he did Hillel, the old, wise ruler of the synagogue in Jerusalem. Although they had known each other for years, they weren't friends. For one, Hillel was old enough to be Caiaphas's father or perhaps even grandfather. For another, they were different in virtually every way imaginable. Hillel was gracious and kind, slow to anger, and humble beyond measure; the things of this world meant nothing to him while the word of God meant everything. Yet, for all their differences, they did share a similarity: they both devoutly professed a deep love for Jehovah's laws, and neither of them could abide someone who didn't follow them with exactness. For Hillel, that intolerance was probably the single biggest flaw in his character; for Caiaphas, it was simply one of many.

Caiaphas walked up the steps and through the arched entryway of the imposing synagogue. He was alone, walking with eyes down and hands clasped behind his back in deep thought. Turning down a narrow hallway, he continued until he came to a wooden door that stood slightly ajar and paused. He smoothed his robe and cloak, ran his fingers over his beard, and then knocked loudly on the frame, waiting for an invitation to enter.

"Come in," said a raspy voice that was almost too faint to hear.

Caiaphas slowly pushed open the door and entered the room. It was small and damp and musty. Oil lamps stood on stands and along shelves on the wall and burned brightly, bathing the windowless room in soft light. Scrolls of papyrus and leather were everywhere—on shelves, on tables, on chairs. Entering the room always brought back memories to Caiaphas, memories of poring over sacred scripture for hours at a time and struggling to commit it to memory.

"Welcome, Caiaphas," Hillel said, attempting to rise from his chair.

"Please, sir, don't get up," Caiaphas responded as he rushed to the old man's side and gently tried to guide him back down.

Hillel made a feeble attempt at shaking free and continued his effort to stand. "Would you deprive this old man the right to honor the office of the chief high priest when he enters my chamber?"

Caiaphas noted the man's choice of words. Hillel wasn't honoring him as a man, but rather the office he held, and Caiaphas wasn't quite sure if there was a hidden meaning in the old man's choice of words. "Your respect is overwhelming," Caiaphas said as he steadied Hillel.

"You honor me with your presence, but please, take a seat," Hillel said, pointing to a comfortable chair that was free of scrolls. "It is an honor to have you visit. How can I be of assistance to you?"

"Rabbi, I'm here on a very serious matter," Caiaphas said in an ominous tone. "Not only serious but troubling and sad as well."

Hillel showed no reaction to the statement. In his long life, he had seen and experienced so many serious matters that he doubted this one could be something he hadn't encountered many times in the past. "Please, tell me what is so troubling," he said with a gentle smile.

"I'm here concerning Joseph of Arimathea, a man of this synagogue."

"Ah, Joseph—a devout, good man and very just," Hillel said, placing his hands on the table in front of him and interlocking his fingers. "He is a man I respect and admire."

Caiaphas gave a weak smile at the comment and leaned forward in his chair. "He is a man I also have greatly admired . . ." Pausing, he cleared his throat and added, "In the past."

Hillel raised his eyebrows slightly at the statement. "But no longer?"

"Rabbi, yesterday while the Sanhedrin met to discuss the blasphemous claims of Jesus of Nazareth, Joseph loudly proclaimed to the entire assembly that he accepted him as the Messiah."

Caiaphas had expected this news to shock Hillel, but the ancient ruler of the synagogue showed no emotion. After a moment, Hillel leaned back in his chair and let out a sigh. "He isn't alone, you know. Others, many others, have proclaimed a similar belief."

"Yes, Rabbi, but others are not members of the Sanhedrin and so highly respected as Joseph."

"In the past seven days, I have had dozens of fathers, mothers, wives, and husbands come to me because someone they love has accepted Jesus. Each of them wants to know the same thing: Will their loved one be forced to leave the synagogue? Will the ruling council excommunicate him or her?"

Caiaphas studied the expression on Hillel's face in an effort to discern his thoughts. "And I assume you told them all the same thing—they would be excommunicated."

Hillel folded his hands and, placing them in his lap, said patiently, "A third of the people in this synagogue have expressed a belief in Jesus. Many of them have come to show me a withered hand that has been healed, their clean white skin that was once covered in leprosy, or a fevered mind that is at peace. Others who once sat and begged at the city gates because they were crippled or blind came in here walking and seeing. Still others came who were deaf but who can now hear. One couple even brought in a small baby who was deformed at birth but is now perfect. What do I say to them, to those whose sicknesses have been cured and whose lives have been changed?"

Caiaphas listened in stunned silence. He expected Hillel to be willing, even anxious, to excommunicate Joseph, but the man was hedging. "Surely you don't believe Jesus is the Messiah?"

"Of course not," Hillel responded contemptuously. "But if we excommunicate Joseph—which is why you have come to see me, is it not?—then must we not also excommunicate all of the others? Is the same sin in one any less or greater than the same sin in another?"

It was a critical question. Under Jewish law, a sin was a sin, regardless of the station in life of the sinner. If Joseph was excommunicated, then it would follow that everyone, one-third of this man's congregation, would also be excommunicated. If that happened, the money flowing into the synagogue from the remaining members would be less—much less. With less money, it would be difficult—probably impossible—to support Hillel and the ten men who sat on the synagogue's ruling council. It was a dilemma.

A gentle smile formed on Caiaphas' lips. He had anticipated this problem and was prepared to offer a solution. It would take a little effort, but he was confident he could make it happen. "Hillel, you know I have the greatest respect for you and your great wisdom," Caiaphas began, "and with your permission, I would like to suggest some things for you to consider."

Hillel adjusted himself in his chair and raised his hand.

"Please, share with me your thoughts."

"Are there not three levels of punishment available to the ruling council of the synagogue in a case such as this?"

"Of course. There are three levels for every case, Caiaphas," the old ruler said unwearyingly. "You know that."

Caiaphas acknowledged the gentle rebuke, but he proceeded as if he hadn't heard it. "First, you can have the person scourged thirty-nine times. Second, you can forbid the sinner from having any interaction with any member of the synagogue, including his own family members, for thirty days or longer. Finally, the sinner can be totally and absolutely excluded not only from this synagogue, but from every synagogue, forbidding him to have any dealings with any of God's chosen people. The sinner loses all rights both civilly and religiously. He becomes a heathen and a publican."

"Yes, yes, that is all true," Hillel said a bit impatiently. "The ruling council has considered this many times over."

"And what was your decision?" Caiaphas asked.

Hillel leaned back in his chair and let out a sigh. He'd been over this so many times that his mind ached, and he didn't really want to review it again, even if this was the chief high priest of the Sanhedrin. Clasping his hands and putting them in his lap, he said, "In the beginning, in the early days of Jesus's activity, we scourged the believers, male and female alike, thinking that would deter others. It didn't. It had just the opposite effect. People viewed the scourging as a source of pride. They rejoiced that they had been beaten for Jesus's sake."

Caiaphas nodded but said nothing. He knew of the scourging. He didn't know of the unexpected results.

"When scourging proved ineffective, we tried temporary excommunication," Hillel continued. "As severe as scourging is, the far greater fear was loss of membership in the synagogue, even if it was temporary. The council decided to make an example, so we excommunicated two people, a man and his wife. They were poor people, the kind most people shun and ignore, but they were vocal. They had a child, a baby girl, that they claimed was born with many deformities. They stood in the synagogue and related to everyone how they took the baby to Jesus and how he supposedly healed the child. After listening to their continual testifying of Jesus, we eventually excommunicated them. The effect was dramatic, but it was only temporary. But this couple testified all the more loudly. Besides that, the number of believers was growing so quickly that we simply couldn't excommunicate them all."

"And what of the third option, total excommunication?" Caiaphas asked.

Hillel shook his head, partly in disbelief at the question. "Come, Caiaphas, surely you know that we would never do that. In all my years in the synagogue, even in the most serious cases, we have never imposed that upon anyone. It is unthinkable!"

"Is it?" Caiaphas asked.

"Yes," Hillel replied flatly.

Caiaphas smiled gently and spoke in the most soothing voice he could muster. "Rabbi, I may have a solution for you. Something that may stem the loss of members from your synagogue without upsetting their, ah, support."

Sensing a possible solution to this heavy dilemma, Hillel leaned forward in his chair. "I'm listening."

"Joseph of Arimathea is one of the most respected men in this great city of Jerusalem. He is one of the most respected members of the Sanhedrin, a man held in high regard and certainly one of—if not the most important—member of your synagogue. And for a man of such stature to stand in front of the Sanhedrin and publicly declare his belief that Jesus is the Messiah is far different, far more serious, than for a mother and father to come to you and declare their belief. If you could make an example of him—of just one single man—in such a way that the other members of the synagogue took notice, would that be of interest to you?"

Hillel looked intently at Caiaphas while he considered what hadn't been said but had been implied: permanently excommunicate Joseph of Arimathea. It was an intriguing thought. Doing so would send the clear message to every member of the synagogue that if the ruling council would excommunicate someone of Joseph's standing, then they would certainly excommunicate lesser people. The fear of total excommunication—not excommunication itself, but the fear of being totally ostracized and immediately changed from being a chosen child of Israel to a heathen—would cause people to rethink their beliefs.

Caiaphas watched Hillel churning things over in his mind and smiled to himself, sure of his success. He knew that Hillel would see to it that Joseph of Arimathea would be the first person to ever be permanently excommunicated from a synagogue.

THIRTEEN

❋ ❋ ❋ ❋ ❋ ❋ ❋ ❋ ❋

"He is from Galilee?" the man asked as he whirled around, his robes billowing from his side. "Why was I not told this before now?"

The small group of men surrounding Pontius Pilate looked at each other, each desperately hoping another would offer some defense for the group's failure to know this important bit of information. After all, they were Pilate's closest advisors—they were supposed to know these things. They were all perplexed how this small bit of information could possibly be useful in the present situation, but none was willing to confess his ignorance. It was only the sudden increase in shouting from below the balcony that momentarily diverted Pilate's attention and saved them from his wrath.

The mob outside was hostile and growing angrier by the minute. It wasn't a large crowd—at least not yet—but what they lacked in size, they made up in volume. At the front of the unruly hoard of men stood Caiaphas, his arms folded across his chest and his chin jutting forward defiantly. He squinted in the bright sunlight as he looked up. There, standing on the same balcony, were the two men he hated most, Pilate and Jesus, and right now he couldn't tell which he hated more. The noise from the crowd assembled behind him was deafening with shouts of "Death!" piercing the air, most coming from priests and rulers in the Sanhedrin. Caiaphas delighted in their outbursts and wished there was some way he could amplify their threats, thereby increasing the pressure on Pilate to pass a death sentence on Jesus. Death was the only way to stop this man who rocked the very foundation of his religion and made Caiaphas's life so miserable with his teachings.

"If he is a Galilean, is it not Herod's responsibility to judge him?" Pilate asked, and this time he was expecting an answer.

Everyone in the group was terrified of the man they served. His temper and unpredictable mood swings had resulted in more than one of their number being exiled or killed. Only because he had the misfortune of standing nearest to Pilate and being the focus of his glare did a dour little man finally speak up. "Yes, Excellency, he should rightly be judged by Herod," he said in a shaky voice.

Suddenly, it was as if each of the men came to the same realization and understood why Pilate was relieved to learn Jesus was from Galilee. It was an ingenious solution. Sending Jesus to Herod for judgment would allow Pilate to remove himself from this controversial situation, a situation that in Pilate's mind was destined to grow much worse.

Pilate walked to the edge of the balcony and held his hands in the air, signaling to the crowd that he wished to speak and needed silence. As the roar of the crowd died to a low murmur, Pilate spoke, "You men of Judah, I have interviewed this man at length. Whatever his claims or his object may be, I find nothing in him worthy of death."

The last part of what he said was completely lost in the angry shouts of the mob. The force of the reaction caused Pilate to involuntarily pull back from the railing. He anxiously turned to both his right and left to confirm that a collection of soldiers still stood at their posts, ready to fight off the priests should they storm the balcony. Holding his hands in the air in an attempt to restore order, Pilate looked directly at Caiaphas, as if pleading for help. But Caiaphas stood motionless, a thin smile on his lips; he was enjoying this scene and had no intention of doing anything to calm the crowd's anger.

Pilate shouted over the roar of the crowd. No one could hear what he was saying, but those below him could see his lips moving and slowly tried to calm those around them so they could hear what he was saying. Eventually, a nervous quiet settled over the mob, which allowed Pilate to speak.

"This man, Jesus, is a Galilean. By the laws of Rome, he should rightfully be judged of Herod Antipas, tetrarch of Galilee, and not me," he managed to say before a few loud hoots and hollers erupted from the crowd.

These were met with shouts: "Quiet, listen to what he is saying!"

"This day, Herod is in Jerusalem at his palace. I will send Jesus to him for judgment." Before the mob could react, Pilate walked from the balcony to the security of the fortress. Turning to the same dour man who had spoken, Pilate said, "You will see that the Galilean is immediately taken to Herod. You are to explain to him the situation and remain until he passes judgment. Only then are you to return and bring me word of his decision. Do you understand?"

The little man nodded, emboldened by his sudden new responsibility. He pointed to three others in the group and said, "Come with me." The four of them turned back to the balcony where Jesus remained standing in complete silence. Motioning to several of the guards, the little man said, "You, there! By Pilate's orders we are to take this man to Herod's palace. Form a barrier around us and clear the way as we walk. If anyone gets in the way or attempts to stop us, use whatever force is necessary to ensure our safety and the delivery of this man."

FOURTEEN

The dour little man had done exactly as he had been commanded. He had taken Jesus to Herod for judgment, but the exchange had been brief—too brief—and now he was forced to report back. He stood outside the chamber door, his nerves so tense his stomach was twisted in knots. Sweat bubbled up on his forehead like water from a spring. His sleeve was long since wet from wiping the drops of water that had slid down his forehead and stung his eyes. Never had he experienced such anxiety and stress. A drop of sweat oozed from his hairline, raced between his eyebrows, and coasted to a stop at the tip of his large nose. He swiped at it with his fingers, amazed that he could even have any sweat left in him.

He stood alone, abandoned by his three associates who had accompanied him to Herod's palace with Jesus. Returning from Herod, he had begged each of the men to stay with him when he reported back to Pilate, but they had insisted that Pilate had commanded him, and him alone, to make the report of what happened to Jesus. *Cowards! They are all cowards*, the little man thought.

Fear entirely overcame him when the door opened and a slave motioned for him to enter. Only by steadying himself on the doorframe did he keep his knees from collapsing as he took the first step. The slave turned back and gave the man an annoyed looked, but did nothing to assist him. After a brief pause, the man straightened up and managed to take a step, and then another, and another, until he was standing in the middle of the room.

Pontius Pilate sat in the corner of the room, perched on a richly colored purple couch piled high with yellow and white silk pillows. In front of him was a small table covered with fruit, cheese, and bread, with a lone silver goblet on one corner. To the man's surprise, nobody else was in the room. Even the slave who had shown him in had somehow disappeared. The two of them were alone, and it made him quake even more.

"Gaius Didius," Pilate said pleasantly, the irritation of a few hours earlier completely gone. "Do you have news for me of Jesus?"

The little man swallowed hard, knowing the words he was about to speak could well be some of his last. He couldn't resist wiping his sweat, but rather than using his sleeve as he was prone to do, he raised his right hand and with a quick swipe, mopped the sweat with his fingertips, where it immediately dripped on the floor at his feet.

He had rehearsed a thousand times during the long walk from Herod's palace back to Pilate's fortress exactly what he was going to say. With each step he refined and improved his speech so that by the time he reached the fortress it was perfect. And now he stood in front of Pilate, unable to recall a single word.

When Didius didn't immediately respond, Pilate raised his eyebrows. "Well, what news do you have?" He picked up a knife, sliced a piece of cheese, and put it in his mouth.

The little man's eyes focused on the blade of the knife. He was so seized by fear that he began talking in a single long sentence at a furious pace. "Your Excellency most noble Pontius Pilate we did as you directed we delivered this man Jesus to

Herod and Caiaphas renewed his accusations and members of the Sanhedrin supported his claims then Herod aggressively questioned the man and tried to determine his guilt or innocence—"

Pilate held up the hand that held the knife. "I can't understand what you're saying. Tell me again, this time more slowly, what happened."

The little man took a deep breath and spoke more slowly, but with no less apprehension. "We did as you directed. We delivered Jesus to Herod for judgment. Caiaphas and all the members of the Sanhedrin renewed their accusations and even produced people to support their claims. Herod aggressively questioned the man and tried to determine his guilt or innocence."

"What did Jesus say?" asked Pilate as he laid the knife on the table.

Seeing the knife back on the table calmed the little man, and he said with slightly more assurance, "Nothing!"

Pilate sat upright. "Nothing? The man said nothing in his defense?"

"Yes, Excellency. He stood in complete silence."

"What did our friend Herod do?" Pilate asked, his voice filled with sarcasm, because he did not like Herod.

"He was irritated at Jesus's lack of response and his continued silence, so Herod mocked him by calling him a king and placed a luxurious robe on him."

"And then?" Pilate asked.

What little confidence Gaius Didius Dento had gained in the last minute suddenly vanished, and he felt his knees getting weak. His head became light as he replied, "And then he demanded that I return him to you for judgment."

Pilate exploded off the couch and hurled the table and food across the room. The little man ducked, covering his head with his hands and arms, but there was no need. The table landed well short of him and the cheese and bread flew far to his side, slamming into a side wall and bouncing harmlessly to the floor. The honey-coated figs and dates followed the trajectory of the other food but rather than bouncing off the walls, they stuck and slowly slid to the floor. Only the knife found a home. Its blade sunk deep in the wooden frame surrounding a window.

"He *what?*" Pilate bellowed at the same instant guards came bursting into the room with swords drawn.

Had Dento not been huddled on the floor with his hands and arms over his head, any one of the three guards might have instantly sliced him in half, thinking he was a threat to the man they protected. As it was, they surrounded him with their swords, lightly poking his arms and back, their razor-sharp tips drawing little specks of blood that stained his robe.

Pilate strode up to Dento and grabbed him by the hair on the back of his head, forcing him to his feet. "Tell me *exactly* what happened," he said, letting go of the man's sweat-streaked hair and wiping his hand on the man's robe.

Shaking as he was, Dento had a difficult time talking, and he began jabbering incoherently. Pilate gripped the man by his shoulders. "I promise that no harm will come to you, but you must speak slowly and tell me everything."

Hearing Pilate's assurance that he wasn't about to be run through with a sword, the man sucked in a lungful of air and recounted the entire episode. Only twice did Pilate interrupt him for more details.

"Where are Caiaphas and his band of agitators now?" Pilate asked Dento after he finished.

"They are gathering outside the balcony, Excellency," Dento said. And then feeling bolder, he added, "They tormented us all the way from Herod's palace, growing more numerous and more hostile as we came. They are growing angrier and more demanding each minute."

"And where is Jesus? What have you done with him?"

"He is being held by the guards in a small room here in the fortress."

Pilate let out a sigh, his shoulders slumping, as he considered all that he been told. Dento and the three guards stood in the center of the room and exchanged anxious glances as Pilate walked silently to a chair and sat down. He rested his elbows on the arms of the chair and put his fingertips to his mouth as he absentmindedly kicked at a slab of bread that lay on the ground near his foot.

The long silence was interrupted by a soft knock at the door. Pilate motioned to one of the guards, and he walked over and opened it. A diminutive slave girl holding a small silver tray brushed past the burly soldier. Stepping over bits of cheese and bread, she walked to where Pilate sat and held out the tray for him. On the tray was a single small piece of parchment folded neatly in half. Pilate smiled weakly at the girl as he removed the parchment from the tray and dismissed her with a wave of his hand. He unfolded the parchment, read what it said, and then slumped forward in the chair, resting his elbows on his knees. He reread the note, slowly opened his fingers, and then let it drop to the floor.

Standing up, Pilate took a deep breath of air and turned to the guards. "Go get Jesus and bring him to the balcony." Then turning to Gaius Didius Dento, he said, "You are coming with me; we are going to the balcony to settle this matter of Jesus for good."

FIFTEEN

❋ ❋ ❋ ❋ ❋ ❋ ❋

Joseph stood alone, gazing down from his isolated hillside perch at the small group of people clustered at the base of the middle of the three crosses. Slightly beyond them, three Roman soldiers were engaged in intense conversation as they examined a beautiful white robe woven entirely without seams. The distance made it impossible for him to hear what anyone was saying, and Joseph thought it was just as well—he preferred the quiet solitude as he watched.

Joseph lifted his eyes from the two huddled groups of people to the horizon where storm clouds were amassing to the east. The clouds were building rapidly and forming into tall towers that billowed white against the bright blue spring sky. Looking at the thickening clouds made Joseph conscious that the light breeze that had been blowing in his face for the past hour had now shifted and was blowing stronger from his right. "A storm is coming," he mumbled to himself as he gathered his light cloak about him. He momentarily thought about the discomfort of sitting in the rain, but then harshly chastised himself for having such a petty thought. Being soaked by rain melted to utter insignificance compared to the pain the man hanging on the middle cross was experiencing.

For two hours Joseph had stood, keeping his lonely vigil,

watching as people passed by the crosses. The small group that stood there now had been present the entire time, but more, many more, had passed on their way to or from the gates of Jerusalem. Some pointed and laughed, mocking the man who hung in the middle, suspended on the cross with spikes in his hands and feet. Others paused to bow in reverence and then slipped quickly away. A third group, by far the majority, passed by with little more than a glance, too preoccupied with their troubles or too frightened to look.

A splat of moisture on the bridge of Joseph's nose caused him to gaze up at the sky once again. Only a few moments before, the billowing white clouds were far in the distance. Now the clouds, growing darker and thicker, and just beginning to spit drops of rain, surrounded Jerusalem and the entire countryside. It wasn't only the clouds whose pace was quickening; the soldiers also grew more anxious. Even from his distance, Joseph could see they had somehow drawn lots for the seamless white robe because one of them tossed his head back in laughter. Rolling the robe as tightly as possible, he stuffed it beneath his tunic.

The afternoon sunlight that had warmed Joseph's back suddenly disappeared, blotted out by the immense mass of thick gray clouds that swirled in uncontrolled commotion and overshadowed the city, bathing it and the countryside in an eerie shade of gray. There was no lightning or thunder, but Joseph knew it was only a matter of time.

The darkness of the afternoon turned darker still as the clouds became black. As if taking a cue from the weather, each of the three soldiers picked up a large hemlock club and walked to a cross. Without hesitation, the first soldier grasped his club in both hands and, swinging it in a wide arc with all his might, slammed it into the left leg of the man hanging on the cross nearest Joseph. The man's body jolted from the force of the impact, and his shin bone shattered, ripping through the flesh.

As blood dripped down, the soldier shifted his position and swinging with even more intensity, repeated the movement, shattering the bone in the man's right leg. The man lurched on the cross, but his screams of agony were lost in the wind.

The second soldier walked to the cross farthest from Joseph and duplicated the actions of the first. The club connected solidly with the other man's shin bone, but while the bone cracked, it didn't shatter. Backing off slightly, he again swung the heavy club, this time with far more force and embedded it in the man's leg. The man writhed in pain as the soldier wrenched the club free and took aim at the other leg. Two more swings, and the second leg was shattered. Blood oozed down his legs and dripped from his toes.

The third soldier, the man who had won the white robe, walked to the middle cross and was poised to do as his two companions had done but hesitated. Looking up at the limp body hanging on the cross, he dropped his club to the ground and walked over to a high rock overhang that jutted out from the hill where he hefted the shaft of a long spear. Returning to the cross, he walked to the side of the man and grasped the spear with both hands. With a loud yell and one swift movement, he thrust the bronze tip upward. The force of his movement sent the spearhead and six inches of the shaft into the man's body. Countless battles had taught the soldier exactly what to do next, and he violently shook the shaft in an effort to damage as many internal organs as possible. Stepping back so as not to get covered with blood and body parts, he yanked the shaft from the body and looked on as fluid gushed from the wound. At that exact instant, a massive bolt of lightning flashed across the sky, causing the soldier to drop his spear in the dirt and run for the shelter of the rock overhang.

The intense whiteness of the lightning lit up the entire countryside, and Joseph involuntarily ducked his head and turned from the scene below him. The crash of the thunder that accompanied it instinctively caused him to clasp his hands over his ears, but he was too slow. His eardrums rebelled at the roar, and his ears rang as the thunder reverberated through the air. Joseph slumped to his knees beside a massive olive tree and pulled his cloak tightly around his shoulders. The huge tree trunk, thick as it was, offered scant protection from the vicious sting of the sand that a ferocious wind hurtled through the air. It was then that the Supreme God of Heaven and earth unleashed a storm unlike any other.

Bright flashes of lightning ripped through the sky and struck the earth ceaselessly. Cracks of thunder rattled the ground with such intensity that Joseph was certain the earth would split beneath him. And then the rain and hail fell. It came in furious sheets, stripping the leaves from the olive tree under which he hunkered, stinging his body. Battered, Joseph stood and tried running for the protection of another tree, but the ground beneath his feet was already awash in mud and flowing rain water, making the hillside treacherously slippery. Joseph lost his footing and careened headfirst down the hillside in a torrent of water and mud. Bumping against rocks and tree stumps, he came to a stop next to a hollow log, where he clawed his way inside.

Joseph shivered in his cramped hovel and waited as the storm lashed the countryside. Time passed with excruciating slowness as the thunder and lightning repeatedly flashed and cracked all around him. The rain continued falling with such fury that he expected to be washed out of his makeshift shelter. He had no idea how long he was holed up nor what time of day it was, but he knew that the Sabbath was approaching, and if he was going to do what he knew he must, he had no choice but to do it now, so he backed his way out of the log into the torrential downpour.

Slipping and sliding, he managed to slowly creep down to a small trail that traversed the hillside. It was awash in debris, and gullies bisected it at irregular intervals, making walking difficult. The rain's intensity decreased slightly, and he managed to pick up his pace as the trail gradually began its descent to the main road into Jerusalem. Ordinarily the road would be crowded with people making their way to or from the city, and travel would be slow. Now, though, the storm had driven people to whatever shelter they could find, and he had the road to himself. Walking, sometimes jogging, he made his way through the muddy streets to his destination.

SIXTEEN

The small ante-room was empty, save for the rain-soaked Joseph. His cloak and shawl had done nothing to stop the rain, and he now stood with little droplets of water cascading from his clothes. They mixed with the water that drizzled off his hair and beard and gathered in a puddle on the floor around his soaked and muddy sandals. At another time, under different circumstances, he would be embarrassed to be seen like this in public, but not now, not today, and not with everything that had gone on in the past two days. Though he was meeting with a powerful person, his appearance was not a consideration to him.

The slave had ushered him into the room, and in a voice barely above a whisper, he had bid Joseph to remain standing. He hadn't offered him any refreshment or even a towel or rag to dry himself, a not-so-subtle reminder that in this place, Jews were not welcome.

"Joseph of Arimathea?" the feminine voice from behind him said cautiously. "This is an odd surprise. What brings you here?"

Although half expecting it, the voice startled him, and Joseph whirled around and sent a shower of water flying from his cloak, which splashed onto the woman's lavender robes.

Bowing his head out of respect for the woman, Joseph said, "Thank you for seeing me, Procula. It is very considerate of you."

She dismissed the comment with a wave of her hand. "After all you did for me during the past year, this is nothing," she said. It was a reference to the extraordinary efforts to which Joseph had gone six months earlier to obtain some very rare and costly spices and incense for her palace in Caesarea.

Other Jewish merchants refused to deal with her out of hatred for her husband. At first, Joseph had taken the same position, but when she personally came to his business, rather than sending one of her slaves, and practically begged him to help her, he acquiesced. He reasoned that her money was as good as anyone's and had made a handsome profit on each transaction. Besides, he found her to be a much better person than the gossipmongers said she was. Still, after each meeting, he wondered how such a considerate woman could endure being the wife of Pontius Pilate.

It was during their second, or maybe the third meeting, that she made a casual remark about a Galilean named Jesus. Had Joseph ever heard of the man, she asked innocently. The question took him by surprise. Here was the wife of a powerful Roman procurator asking about a Jewish religious figure, and Joseph had been cautious.

Uncertain of the reason for her question, Joseph responded vaguely. He told her that he knew only what others were saying, but he knew nothing personally. She confided that she knew little of him as well. During their last meeting, though, she brought up Jesus again, this time with far more enthusiasm. The depth of her understanding of his teachings both amazed and surprised Joseph. Not that the woman knew the doctrine in detail, but she had far more than a casual knowledge of the man and his teachings. Joseph made a mental note of her interest, but they never met again, so there was no further conversation.

"Procula," he stated bluntly, "I came here seeking your help in something very important to me."

She raised her eyebrows and cautiously said, "And that is?"

Joseph knew the next few words he spoke could either condemn or help him. And once spoken, there would be no retreating—not that he intended to do so. If he was unsuccessful, he wasn't sure what he would do because there was no other course of action open to him.

He wasn't quite certain where to begin, but with the hours slipping away and the Sabbath approaching, he decided to be blunt. "Do you recall our conversations about a man named Jesus?" he asked.

Her reaction surprised him. At the mention of Jesus, Procula's body visibly tensed.

"Yes," she replied, keeping her voice noncommittal.

"He was . . ." Joseph hesitated. He was about to say, "sentenced by your husband to be crucified earlier today," but simply said, "He was crucified earlier today." He waited for a reaction, any reaction that would let him know how she felt about Jesus. There was nothing. She just stood silently, so he quietly added, "I have come to ask your husband for his body."

Procula stared at Joseph, her dark eyes showing a suspicious curiosity. Joseph could not read the emotion in her face. Had he been wrong? Was she not a believer? The silence in the small room was awkward, and Joseph shifted his weight from one leg to the other.

"And you came to me, hoping I would convince my husband to give you the body?" she said, with anxiety in her voice.

"No!" Joseph exclaimed. "I came only to see if you would intervene on my behalf to get me the opportunity to talk with Pilate myself."

"What makes you think I can be of assistance?"

Joseph looked at the woman. "I don't know if you can. But you are the only person I know who has access to your husband, and I'm seeking a favor."

"I see," she said, still not showing any hint of her belief in Jesus. Then there was a pause, a very long pause. Taking a deep breath, she finally said, "I tried to intercede in Jesus's behalf, you know."

Joseph gulped, shocked at what she said. Trying not to appear too surprised, he simply said, "I was not present at his trial. I didn't know of your efforts to secure his release."

Brushing her hand through her hair and moistening her lips with her tongue, she continued, "When I heard Jesus had been brought to Pilate, I sent him a note begging my husband not to have anything to do with the man. I told him Jesus was an innocent and righteous person, not the evil man that Caiaphas and the Sanhedrin made him out to be."

"That was extremely risky of you," Joseph interjected.

Procula nodded in agreement. "I truly believe my husband wanted to let him go, but he was trapped by that wretched Herod and especially Caiaphas and Annas and your fellow members of the Sanhedrin."

Joseph looked at her, believing in her efforts to intercede on behalf of Jesus but unwilling to accept her seeming attempt to excuse Pilate's involvement in the crucifixion. Knowing time was working against him, he gathered his cloak more tightly around him to ward off the chill from the rain. "He is dead. I have come to ask Pilate for his body."

Procula was stunned at his announcement. "He is dead? So quickly?"

"I was there," Joseph continued. "I watched them drive the spikes in his hands and feet. I have stood these past hours near the cross, waiting for him to die. And now I have come to ask—beg, if necessary—that Pilate allow me to remove his body from the cross and prepare it for burial."

This time it was Procula who was amazed. "Are you a believer?"

"Yes," Joseph said flatly.

"But you're a member of the Sanhedrin. Were not all of you opposed to Jesus?"

"Most, but not all," Joseph replied. "There are a few of us who believe and accept Jesus as the Messiah."

"But why you, Joseph? Where are his disciples and apostles? Why have they not come for his body?"

Joseph had no answer to these questions. "With the exception of John, none of his apostles were at the crucifixion. Other than him, there was only Jesus's mother, Mary of Magdalla, and a few other women present."

Procula mulled this piece of news over in her mind. "You too are taking an enormous risk by your actions. Caiaphas and Annas will crush you when they learn of your true beliefs and what you plan to do now."

"They already know," he said. "Besides, you took a risk by attempting to defend him. Was it worth it to you?"

"My risk and the results that follow are nothing compared to what you will experience. You will be cast out of the Sanhedrin and excommunicated from the synagogue," she said in an even tone. "You will be outcast from society. Not only that, they will do everything they can to destroy your business and probably your life as well. They will crush you," she said, her voice growing firmer as if issuing a warning.

Joseph had already weighed these issues in his mind countless times. "Perhaps," Joseph said. "But I have asked myself a dozen times as I walked from Golgotha to this fortress if I truly believe that Jesus is the Messiah. I am here because I believe that he is, and if I must choose between my belief and my wealth, I will stand by my beliefs."

Procula stared at Joseph, impressed with his courage. "What would you like me to do?"

"Arrange for me to meet with Pilate. As soon as possible. Right now, in fact," Joseph said urgently.

Procula looked intently at Joseph as if trying to decide what to do. "It may not be a pleasant experience for you, Joseph, meeting with my husband," she warned. "You know only too well that he dislikes Jews, especially members of the Sanhedrin."

Joseph considered her words and almost chuckled to himself. In the last two days, he'd already faced the wrath of the Sanhedrin, his wife had given him an ultimatum of divorce, and his friends had deserted him. What could this Roman possibly say that would make things any worse?

"I will do what I have to do," he said slowly and deliberately.

Procula realized that the man before her was truly good. "Wait here," she commanded. Then quickly turning around, she said, "I will talk with him, and you shall have your meeting. And may your God bless you in what you say and how you say it."

Only a few moments later, a slave boy, no more than twelve or thirteen years old, ushered Joseph into the large hall. The boy stopped halfway across the expansive tile floor and motioned for Joseph to also stop. They stood silently for a moment, and then without warning the boy left, leaving Joseph alone, looking across the large hall at the backs of two men.

One man, the shorter of the two, was dressed in a flowing white robe that hung loosely on his shoulders. Even from this distance, Joseph could see it was of costly fine-twined linen. It was held in place by a belt, more of a girdle really, that encircled his waist. His feet were shod with richly appointed leather sandals of a type Joseph had rarely seen, obviously made by craftsmen in a distant land. Although he could only see the back of the man's head, Joseph could see that his once dark brown hair now contained equal amounts of gray, and a growing bald spot was evident. Age had obviously taken its toll on the man—where once he had been a warrior, his body now reflected the effects of too many banquets filled with rich food and too little physical exercise.

The second man was a centurion, taller and in much better physical condition. Clasped at each shoulder and hanging down his back almost to the floor was a bright red cloak. Joseph had seen far too many centurions in his life, and he knew that when this one turned around, he would have brightly shined body armor around his chest and abdomen. He also knew there would be a sword dangling in a sheath at his side. He could tell from the bulge coming from under the left side of the cloak that the centurion held his helmet in the crook of his left arm.

The two men were obviously in conversation, but they were too far away for Joseph to hear what they were saying. Whatever it was, they were looking out the window and seemed to pay him no attention. For a moment he wondered if they knew he was standing there but quickly dismissed the thought. With the noise his footsteps had made as he walked across the hall, it would be impossible not to know.

With his back still to Joseph, the shorter of the two men called out, "What do you want, Joseph of Arimathea?"

The centurion turned to eye Joseph with a suspicious gaze. Joseph returned the man's glare but said nothing—he wasn't quite sure how to proceed. He had never met Pontius Pilate, or even seen him up close, but his deeds and reputation stirred hatred in Joseph's heart and the heart of every other Jew.

As procurator of all Judea, he was Caesar's resident governor, the man charged with collecting the taxes, maintaining the peace, and enforcing the law, and he did it all with treachery and brutality. As Joseph stood there, his mind raced back over Pilate's bloody reign. Hundreds of innocent Jews had been hacked to death by soldiers because they rebelled when Pilate tried to use sacred synagogue funds to build an aqueduct. And though Joseph had no use for Samaritans, he still pitied them when Pilate brutally attacked their cities for no reason.

The thought of these and countless other incidents increased Joseph's distaste and emboldened him.

"I've come to Pilate with a request," Joseph said in a forceful yet calm voice.

"So my wife informed me," he replied, his back still to Joseph. Joseph knew his refusal to turn around was meant to show disrespect, to convey the message that Pilate was holding this audience at the insistence of his wife. He did not need to condescend to talking with Jews, even if this one was an especially wealthy member of the Sanhedrin. "What is it you want?" he asked gruffly.

"I've come asking Pilate for the body of Jesus of Nazareth," he said boldly. "Whom you ordered crucified earlier today."

Pilate spun around, his robe swirling out in an arc as he did so. "You *what?*" he bellowed, both incredulous and confused at the request. "Why would you, a member of the Sanhedrin, come here begging the body of that man?"

Joseph stood motionless, considering. It was a fair question. Why exactly was he here? Joseph took a deep breath and squared his shoulders. "I believe in the doctrine he taught," he proclaimed.

The response took Pilate by complete surprise. "You, a Pharisee, believed in this man Jesus?" he retorted.

"Yes!"

Pilate considered the response with skepticism. The man had courage—Pilate had to give him that—but it was truly bizarre that one of his position and stature would choose to follow Jesus. But, he reasoned, his wife had been taken in by this Jesus and had become a believer, so why not a Pharisee? The entire situation was troubling, and Pilate inwardly fretted that the death of Jesus would hardly be the end of the matter.

"This whole province has been turned upside down by Jesus of Nazareth," he said. "The next thing I'll hear is that my centurion here, Lucretius Cato, has become a believer in Jesus's doctrines."

If the centurion was surprised by the question, he didn't show it. Without the slightest hesitation, he said, "Two years ago, before I was promoted to my current position in your service, I had a servant who was extremely ill of palsy, so sick he was almost to die. I knew of Jesus's teachings and the many miracles he had performed, so I traveled to Capernaum to ask Jesus to heal my servant. He did so without ever even seeing the boy."

"Then you too believe he is the Jews' Messiah?" Pilate asked incredulously of the centurion.

"Whether he is the Messiah of which they speak, I don't know. But this much is true: my servant was sick, and Jesus healed him," the centurion said, looking at Pilate and then at Joseph.

Pilate slowly shook his head in disbelief as he walked to the edge of the room and slumped into a high-backed chair covered in gold. It had been a long day filled with hatred, strife, and bitterness. More than that, it had been filled with confusion, and now in the last few minutes Pilate had become even more confused.

Folding his arms across his chest, Pilate looked first at the centurion and then Joseph, as if trying to make sense of everything he had heard and witnessed in the past several hours concerning Jesus. One minute, two, then three passed as he sat in silence.

Unfolding his arms and rising from the chair, Pilate looked at Joseph and asked skeptically, "Is he dead already?" He asked this knowing that people who were crucified could hang on the cross in agony for days before finally dying.

"Yes, he is," said Joseph.

Looking at the centurion, Pilate asked, "Can this be true?"

"The Sabbath is quickly approaching, and the chief priests

insist that he and the two thieves with him be dead and off the cross before then. We have broken the legs of the thieves, but when the soldiers came to Jesus, he was already dead. To be certain, one of them pushed a spear through his side. He is dead!"

Pilate considered this for a long moment. Then walking directly in front of Joseph, he said simply, "Go! You may have the body of your Messiah." He turned away from Joseph, slowly walked across the hall in silence, and peered out the window.

Joseph turned and started toward the doorway through which he had entered. The centurion called after him, "I will notify my men that you will be coming for the body."

SEVENTEEN

The rain falling from the dark afternoon sky forced Devorah to abandon her secluded spot on the veranda for the shelter and isolation of her sitting room. The gusty wind that preceded the rain had misted her with dust, leaving her face feeling gritty, and she paused at a small table, leaning over a shallow basin of water to wash her face. Her reflection in the smooth clear water shocked her. It shouldn't have. This morning had been the third time she had watched the sun climb above the hills to the east, the third day in a row she had gone with nothing more than a snatch of sleep. For two lonely nights she sleeplessly watched the moon as it tracked across a black sky littered with stars. Last night she hadn't even bothered to get into the empty bed she had once shared with her husband. She had simply wrapped herself in a soft sheepskin blanket and sat on a couch on the veranda.

Her body craved sleep, but her mind wouldn't yield. For three days and two nights, it replayed events from forty years of marriage, and each time, without fail, it always returned her to the words they had exchanged three very long days ago. It was three days since she had seen her husband, and the lack of sleep and increasing stress of these past days was showing itself in deepening lines in her brow and dark circles around her sunken eyes. It was external evidence of internal commotion.

Dipping her hands in the basin, she gingerly splashed water on her face, patted her face dry with a soft yellow cloth, and pinched her cheeks in a fruitless effort to chase away the pallid appearance. Smoothing the wrinkles in her robe, Devorah knew she couldn't go on like this. She must do something, anything, to clear her jumbled mind. She needed to talk, to tell someone what she was thinking and feeling. She needed someone in whom she could confide; someone who would listen and offer consolation; someone who would give support without judgment.

Devorah walked to a comfortable chair in the sitting room and eased herself down, sheltered from the rain pelting the tile roof and the thunder vibrating the walls. The violence of the storm caused her a wry smile—it reflected the turmoil in her heart. That turmoil made it difficult to focus her thoughts on the person to whom she could turn for help. As the thunder rolled, she sat pondering woman after woman—it simply had to be a woman. She mentally went through a list of her friends, dismissing each almost as quickly as she thought of them. And then it came, a sudden flash of inspiration. She knew the exact person who could help guide her through the darkness that engulfed her.

Devorah dashed to her closet and pulled from a peg the first cloak she saw. It was soft but tightly woven and had splashes of green, purple, and orange arranged in bold designs. As she tied it in place with a white sash, she thought how black or dark gray would have been more appropriate colors—either would be a closer reflection of her mood. Lifting a white woven scarf from among the dozens that hung on the rack, she placed it on her head as she strode down the hallway toward the main door of her mansion.

The force of the rain and wind made her gasp as she stepped outside, but pulling her scarf tightly around her chin, she lowered her head and walked with a determined pace across the courtyard toward the gate. Ordinarily she would have exchanged a short but courteous greeting with the servant who stood guard beside the gate, but as she approached all she said was, "I'm leaving for a while. I'm not certain when I will return." The servant acknowledged her comments but said nothing in return as he opened the gate and she stepped out onto the rain soaked avenue.

Within less than a dozen steps, Devorah's dainty leather sandals and feet were caked with mud, and the hem of both her robe and cloak were covered in dirty brown spots from the puddles she unsuccessfully tried to avoid. She silently cursed the rain and pulled the cloak tighter around her neck and shoulders.

Less than a quarter mile separated their homes, and with each step, she churned over in her mind what she would say. Nearing the gate of the home, she called to the huddled servant inside, who was trying unsuccessfully to stay dry in the rain. "Open, please. It is Devorah."

The gate quickly opened, and she thanked the servant as she passed by. Reaching the awning that led to the entrance, she removed the scarf from her head and shook it rapidly to dislodge the drops of rainwater. She stamped her feet as she approached the door, leaving a trail of little mud globs. Her cloak was soaking wet, and the rain had started to penetrate her robe as well. An involuntary shiver coursed through her body.

She stopped at the large oak door and gave three hearty pulls on the thin rope attached to the bronze bell. The clapper slammed against the insides of the bell and sent sounds reverberating through the air. Only a scant moment passed before the door swung open.

"I'd like to see Anna; please fetch her for me immediately," she announced as she brushed passed the young servant girl who stood in the doorway. The girl quickly closed the heavy door to keep out the pelting rain and hurried away without saying anything.

Devorah removed her rain-soaked cloak. Under any other circumstances, she would have chastised the servant for not offering to take if from her and hang it where it could dry, but today, with the burden she carried, it seemed like such an insignificant issue. Draping the wet garment over a hook in the entryway, she nervously rehearsed in her mind what she would say.

"Devorah, you're soaking wet!" Anna exclaimed upon seeing her. Taking Devorah by the arm, she said, "Come, warm yourself by the fire."

The large room they entered was warm and comfortable. The windows had heavy purple drapes pulled across them to keep out the coldness of the rain and wind, but they made the room darker than it normally was at this time of day. The flames from the crackling fire sent shadows dancing across the walls as Anna pulled a large comfortable chair near the fire. "Please, Devorah, sit down and get warm," she said, motioning toward the chair.

"Thank you, Anna," Devorah replied. She walked across the marble floor, leaving still another trail of mud from her sandals as she did so.

"What in Heaven's name brings you out in a storm like this?" Anna asked as she slid a second chair across the floor, placing it so they could sit knee to knee.

Devorah didn't answer the question but forced a slight smile through tightly drawn lips. She folded her hands in her lap, alternately bit at her lower lip, and then pursed her lips tightly together. After a moment had passed in silence, a small tear formed in the corner of Devorah's right eye. It streaked down her cheek and landed on the back of her folded hand. Anna removed a delicate piece of linen cloth from the folds of her robe to wipe the tear away. Leaning forward, she softly dabbed at the tears that were now coming from both eyes.

She shuddered slightly and managed to choke out, "It's Joseph!"

Anna scooped up both of Devorah's hands in her own and anxiously asked, "Is he dead?"

Devorah shook her head back and forth but said nothing.

Is he injured or ill?"

Devorah shook her head again. "No!"

Anna let go of Devorah's hands and sat back in her chair. "Then what is it?" she asked.

Devorah reached into the pocket of her robe, withdrawing her own white linen cloth. Blotting the tears from her eyes and wiping her nose, she said, "It's our marriage."

"What about it?" Anna asked anxiously. "Has he been unfaithful?"

Devorah again shook her head. "Not to me, but to our God."

Anna raised her eyebrow and tilted her head to the side at the curious response. She leaned back deeper in her chair, waiting for the details that she knew would be forthcoming. She didn't have to wait long.

The tears stopped flowing, and Devorah regained her composure. Though bloodshot, Devorah's eyes took on a steely intensity as she exclaimed, "It's that Jesus of Nazareth! Joseph has chosen him over me!"

Anna stiffened at the mention of Jesus but said nothing, waiting for Devorah to continue.

"You know who I'm talking about, of course?" Devorah asked Anna.

"Everyone knows of Jesus of Nazareth," Anna replied calmly.

"He says he first met Jesus two years ago," Devorah began, "and over these last several weeks, there have been nights when he would be out very, very late." Devorah paused briefly as she nervously twisted the linen cloth around her fingers. "At first I didn't know where he was, but I dismissed it, thinking it was something to do with business or matters before the Sanhedrin. But then it became more frequent, and he began changing. Not in a bad way," she said, shaking her head. "If anything, he became a better man."

Anna was perplexed. "And you didn't like that?"

"I approved of the change—it was the reason behind it that troubled me," she replied. "Or more precisely, it was because I didn't know the reason for the change. That's what troubled me."

A look of confusion spread across Anna's face, but all she said was, "I see."

Devorah cleared her throat and continued, "One morning, not long ago, I confronted him."

"Confronted him?" Anna interrupted, this time raising both eyebrows.

"Yes! At first he was evasive, but when I pressured him, he explained he had been meeting with Jesus to learn more of his teachings," Devorah said. She stopped twisting the linen cloth and placed it in her lap. Then leaning forward and resting her elbows on her knees, she said, "Anna, I was dumfounded! Never, ever could I have imaged him or anyone I know listening to Jesus or following his teachings!"

Anna watched Devorah become more agitated as animosity filled her voice.

"I tried to reason with him," Devorah continued, "to explain how much damage it could do to him, to his business, to us, to our place in society, to his position in the Sanhedrin! I went through all of it with him, and in the end, I thought he understood how much we stood to lose by his actions. But then a few nights ago, he came back late again. The next morning, we talked."

"What did he tell you?" Anna asked with genuine interest.

"That he had again met with Jesus and some of his followers."

"And did he tell you of any of his teachings?"

"I don't need to hear about his teachings! That's all everyone talks about. That and the *miracles* he performs," Devorah said with deep sarcasm. "I don't need to cloud my mind with his false teachings or hear wild stories about how he supposedly cures people. His doctrine is blasphemous—surely you know that! He claims he is the Son of God and the Messiah, the one who will deliver us." Pausing only long enough to take a breath, she continued, "As for those miracles, they are shams, nothing more than people his apostles have hired to pretend they have an ailment so he can heal them. They're for show, designed to appeal to simpleminded people and the destitute masses. People like us are not so gullible or easily fooled."

Anna sat motionless in her chair, waiting to hear if her friend had more to say. Devorah interpreted the silence as Anna's agreement and plunged forward. "At the end of our second confrontation, I gave Joseph an ultimatum. I told him he must choose Jesus or me, but he couldn't have both of us."

Shocked, Anna sat upright in her chair. "That, Devorah, may have been unwise," she said cautiously.

Devorah disregarded the remark and continued, "I was so uncertain about what to do that yesterday, in a conversation with my cousin Caiaphas, I told him everything."

"You went to Caiaphas?" Anna asked in disbelief.

Devorah nodded but said nothing for a long moment. Anna watched as yet another change in demeanor swept over Devorah. In a quiet voice, Devorah said, "That's when I learned that Joseph had stood in the Sanhedrin and publicly declared his support for Jesus." And the tears started all over again.

Anna made no effort to reach out to comfort her friend. She settled back in her chair so as to distance herself from Devorah. Resting her arms on the arms of the chair, she watched the tears cascade down Devorah's cheeks and her shoulders shake as she sobbed uncontrollably.

Finally, Devorah regained enough control to blurt out between sobs, "Oh Anna, what am I to do?"

Anna said nothing, waiting for the tears to stop flowing and the sobbing to end. Extending her hand, she offered Devorah her dry linen cloth as a replacement for the crumpled wet one Devorah clutched in her fist. Devorah gratefully accepted the cloth and began dabbing her eyes and wiping her dripping nose.

"Devorah," she said very evenly and without emotion, "I have some things I want to tell you, and I want you to listen carefully." Pausing to ensure she had Devorah's complete attention, Anna took a deep breath. "Some of what I have to say, you may find difficult to understand and maybe even objectionable, but I want you to hear it."

Devorah sat upright, a mixture of confusion and uncertainty on her face, but Anna proceeded in an unwavering voice overflowing with conviction. "I am a believer in Jesus of Nazareth."

Both of Devorah's hands flew to her mouth as she gasped. Her eyes widened in horror. "No!" she screamed in total disbelief.

Anna looked Devorah straight in the eye and nodded. Not a slight tilt of the head, but a distinct, almost exaggerated up and down motion. Anna wanted there to be no ambiguity about her belief. When she was certain Devorah understood, she said, "Not me only, but Nicodemus also."

The shock was too much for Devorah. Her shoulders sagged, and she slumped back in her chair, her arms falling limply to her side. She stared at Anna in complete disbelief. She had come hoping to find solace and peace, and instead she found more confusion. She suddenly felt lost and alone.

"How could you be duped?" Devorah asked with pity in her voice.

"How can you be blind to the truth?"

"Truth?" Devorah asked. "What is truth? All around me is confusion. My husband has chosen Jesus over me. My best friend and her husband have also become believers. Where does that leave me?" Devorah asked earnestly.

"At a crossroads," Anna responded somberly. "But before you choose which road you will take, you owe it to yourself—and to your husband—to at least learn more of this man from Galilee."

In stunned silece, Devorah weighed what had just been said. Did she really owe it to herself or her husband to learn more about Jesus? Why? What could she possibly gain from exploring the teachings of Jesus? The questions raced through her mind, but she had no answers. What she did know, though, was that she desperately wanted rest for her mind and peace for her heart. Looking up at Anna, she said softly, "And who will teach me?"

EIGHTEEN

Joseph ran from Pilate's fortress and onto the streets of Jerusalem. Although the street had rivulets of water flowing down it, he was thankful the rain had slowed to nothing more than a springtime shower. Looking up and down the street, he searched his mind to recall where the nearest cloth merchant was in this part of the city. He could think of two, and they were both in opposite directions. Taking a chance, he started in a fast walk toward the nearest.

People were slowly crawling out of the shelters that had protected them from the storm and were again taking to the streets, causing Joseph to dodge both people and puddles as he hurried along. In fifteen minutes, he came to the side alley where the cloth merchant had his shop. Joseph's heart sank as he strode to the small shop. Its bolted doors and covered windows told him it was unlikely anyone was there, but he still banged on the door and yelled for someone to open. After scraping his knuckles raw from rapping on the stout wooden door, he gave up and headed back onto the streets, chastising himself for the time he had lost.

Doubling back, Joseph slogged through the mud at a trot until he thought his lungs would burst and his legs would collapse. Only then did he slow to a walk. Once he regained his breath, he pushed himself to a run. Rounding a final corner, he looked up the street and was relieved to see a diminutive man in front of a shop, sweeping water and mud away from the door. Pieces of bright cloth on a rope that stretched across the front of the shop fluttered in the light breeze, and Joseph knew the cloth merchant was open for business in spite of the havoc the storm had created.

Setting aside the usual formalities, Joseph entered the shop and hurriedly explained what he wanted. "Ah, you're in luck, my friend. I have exactly what you seek and at a very good price," the man said and shuffled off to find the bolts of material.

Joseph hurried from the cloth merchant's shop with two bundles of cloth tucked securely beneath his mud-caked cloak. The first bundle was a dark brown, coarsely woven cloth that hardly needed protection from the rain. The second, however, was fine white linen, soft to the touch and beautifully woven. The effort of tucking the bundles under his cloak made little sense considering the inside of his cloak was almost as mud-streaked and dirty as the outside, but he felt an overwhelming need to protect the cloth in some fashion.

Turning onto the main street, Joseph moved as quickly as his tired legs and aging body would allow. Getting the cloth had taken much longer than he expected, and now time was against him. Jewish law dictated the bodies be removed from the cross before the Sabbath began at sundown, and if he wasn't there in time, he knew that in spite of the orders from Pilate's centurion, the soldiers would deal with the lifeless body of Jesus with the same calloused disregard as the bodies of the two thieves who had hung beside him. The thought caused Joseph to shudder; it was something he could not allow to happen.

As he ascended the small hill of Golgotha, the slight incline combined with the mud from the violent rainstorm made walking difficult. He slipped several times and half expected the bundles to dislodge from beneath his cloak and land in the mud, but it didn't happen. As he crested the hill, relief and anxiety washed over him at the same time.

Two crosses were lying on the ground, the bodies removed, but the middle of the three crosses remained upright, still bearing its human burden. The body was limp, knees bent, and head titled forward with chin resting on chest. Its entire weight hung from the iron spikes protruding from the torn flesh in his palms. As he walked the last few steps toward the cross, reality struck. In the rush of the past several hours, he never once considered how he alone could remove the body from the cross. His mind raced for a solution, but all he had were questions. Where were the soldiers, those who had nailed him to the cross? What had become of them? And what of the others—Jesus's mother, brothers, apostles, and other followers? Where were they? Was no one available to help? Must he do this alone?

Joseph looked to the west and stole a quick glance at the sun. The thick black clouds that had shielded it were just now drifting apart, and thin ribbons of late afternoon sunlight streaked from the heavens. However he was going to remove the body, he knew he had little time. It wasn't only removing the body that pressed on him—he must clean it and place it in the tomb before sunset. *How terrible,* he thought, *that this brutal business must be finished so the sanctimonious Jews can begin their Sabbath without concern for offending God.*

Joseph turned his gaze to the body hanging on the cross. He reached inside his cloak to remove the bundles. Seeing a small bush a few yards away, he walked over and first draped the coarse brown cloth over the branches and then carefully placed the white linen cloth on top of it. Though the bush bowed under the weight of the cloth, its small branches were stout enough to keep their cargo from hitting the muddy and wet ground. Next, he removed his cloak and let it drop in a

crumpled pile next to the bush. It was already so splattered
with mud that there was no need to worry about it getting
dirty. And then he turned to face the cross and his unpleasant
task.

It was then he saw the lone figure coming toward him from
behind a clump of trees that stood on the far edge of the hill.
With the sun in his eyes, it was impossible to tell who it was,
but the man walked steadily forward until he was just a short
distance away. "Joseph."

Relief swept over Joseph. He ran the few feet that separated them. "Nicodemus," he said softly. "My friend!"

The two men embraced at the foot of the cross but said
nothing more as tears of relief ran from the corners of their
eyes. The men wiped their eyes with the cuffs of their robes.
Joseph said evenly, "I have just come from Pilate. He has given
his consent for me to remove Jesus's body."

Joseph was about to ask Nicodemus how he had come to
this place but decided against it. There would be time enough
for that later. Instead he quietly asked, "Will you help me?"

"That's why I am here, Joseph—to help. What shall we
do?"

Before they could move a step, a harsh voice bellowed from
behind them, "Stop! Identify yourself!"

Both turned to see a Roman soldier striding toward them
with a sword in his right hand and a spear extended menacing
forward in the left. "Who are you?" he demanded as he came
to a stop in front of them, the sword tip barely an inch from
Joseph's chest and the spear poking slightly into Nicodemus's
belly.

"I am Joseph of Arimathea," Joseph said calmly. "This is
Nicodemus. We are members of the Sanhedrin." And then
feeling the need to explain, he pointed to the body of Jesus
and added, "I have Pilate's approval to remove this man's body
from the cross."

"Ah," the soldier said, replacing his sword in its sheath and letting the spear drop to his side. "Lucretius Cato, the centurion, sent word to expect you." With an air of authority and in a condescending tone, the soldier said, "You may proceed."

Under other circumstances, both Joseph and Nicodemus would have chastised the soldier for his attitude, but not today, not with so little time and so much to be done. Besides, they might need the help of this man, and Joseph didn't wish to create an enemy.

Joseph called after the man, "Do you have a ladder we can use?"

The soldier turned around with a look of confusion on his face. "Ladder? For what?"

"So I can climb it to remove the body," Joseph said.

A sly grin spread across the soldier's face. "A ladder would do you no good; you could never pull those spikes out while standing on a ladder. Besides, you don't need it." Without saying another word, he walked to the base of one of the crosses that was already on the ground and picked up a stout oak club. Walking to the back side of the cross bearing the body of Jesus, he took a mighty swing at the wooden wedge that supported the base of the cross, which was dropped in the shallow rock cavity after Jesus had been nailed to it. There was a thunderous crack as the club hit the wedge and sent it flying from its place. As it flew, the soldier jumped from behind the cross, and all three men watched as the cross, with the body still attached, teetered briefly before falling backward.

Joseph and Nicodemus stared in horror and disbelief as the body and cross slammed into the wet ground, splattering mud on their faces and robes. The soldier looked at them and laughed. "I told you you didn't need a ladder." Walking back to his rock overhang, he scooped a pair of large pincers from the ground and tossed them through the air. The pincers landed six inches from Joseph's foot. "You can use those to pull the spikes from his hands and feet."

The body of Jesus that had been washed clean by rain now lay ignominiously in mud. Tears formed in Joseph's eyes as he bent over, picked up the pincers, and looked at the lifeless body stilled pinned to the wooden cross. *How much more must this man endure,* he asked himself, *before he receives the love and respect he always deserved?*

The soldier watched as Joseph picked up the pincers and moved to the feet of Jesus. Joseph eyed the pincers in his hand, looked down at the spike, and back at the pincers. Leaning over, he opened the pincers and clamped them around the head of the spike and pulled. Nothing! He tried again, this time leaning back in an attempt to gain more leverage, but still nothing!

In disgust, the soldier walked from his shelter and gave Joseph a slight push to move him out of the way. "Give me those," he said, pointing to the pincers. "I'll show you how to remove one spike, but you'll have to remove the others; I won't help you anymore."

Straddling the cross he clamped the pincers around the spike barely above where it disappeared into the flesh of Jesus's feet. Using the bone in the instep of Jesus's foot for leverage, he pried rather than pulled the spike. It only moved a quarter-inch, but it moved. Joseph looked on, somewhat surprised. It was obvious the soldier had done this many times before. Relaxing the pincers grip on the spike, the soldier slid it along the spike to where it again disappeared in the flesh and pried again. Three more times he repeated the motion before the spike pulled from the wooden cross. Dropping the pincers in the mud, he placed his left hand on the still pinned together feet and grabbed the spike with his right hand. With a single, rapid jerk, he pulled the bloody spike free and let it drop in the mud.

Picking up the pincers, he stepped in front of Joseph and in a self-important tone said, "That is how it is done." Grabbing Joseph's hand, he slapped the pincers in his open palm and walked through the mud back to the shelter.

Joseph swallowed hard in an effort to send the vomit that was rising in his throat back to his stomach as he stepped to where Jesus's right hand was nailed into the wood. He slumped to his knees in the mud and looked at the torn flesh around the rust-laden spike. The sight was more than his stomach could bear and a stream exploded from his mouth.

There was no need for pincers. The weight of Jesus' body hanging on the cross had torn the flesh and muscle, and there was a gaping hole in the palm of his hand. Joseph simply lifted the hand over the head of the spike, leaving the spike protruding from the wood, and gently laid the hand on Jesus's chest. Rising to his feet, he stumbled around the head of the cross and dropped to his knees by Jesus's left hand. This hole was more gaping than the first, and Joseph swallowed hard to keep from vomiting again. Reaching out with both hands, he carefully lifted the mangled hand from the spike and gently placed it atop the other on Jesus's chest.

Joseph sank back on his folded legs in the mud and broke down. Tears gushed from his eyes and flowed over his lips. As he sat there, shoulders shaking, Nicodemus walked up beside him, resting a reassuring hand on his shoulder. "Come, Joseph," he said softly. "We have little time. We must carry his body to the tomb."

Joseph remained motionless, kneeling in the mud, so Nicodemus walked to the small bush on which Joseph had draped the two pieces of cloth. Lifting the white linen cloth from the bush he pulled the coarse brown cloth free of the branches and returned the white cloth to its place. After making certain the linen cloth wouldn't fall into the mud, Nicodemus walked to the body of Jesus and stretched out the brown cloth beside it. Then ever so carefully, stepping to the head of the cross and squatting down, he slipped his hands under Jesus's shoulders and moved the upper part of the body onto the cloth. Moving to the feet, he grasped an ankle in each hand and lifted them over to the cloth as well. Next he straddled the torso, placed a hand on each side of Jesus' waist, and lifted it over.

As Nicodemus straightened up, he said with urgency in his voice, "Joseph, we must go. Now!"

Joseph looked up into Nicodemus' face. Then he silently rose to his feet and walked to where his cloak lay beside the small bush. Picking it up, he shook it twice to dislodge any loose mud and slipped it on. Then, picking up the bundle of white linen, he tucked it securely inside.

Nicodemus walked to the feet of Jesus, quickly bent over, and tightly grabbed a corner of the brown cloth in each hand and straightened up, waiting for Joseph to do the same at the head.

NINETEEN

✳ ✳ ✳ ✳ ✳ ✳ ✳ ✳ ✳

Joseph and Nicodemus stumbled over rocks and debris as they carried the body to the garden tomb, but neither of them would stop or rest—they were too concerned about the importance of their task and the lateness of the hour. As they neared the tomb, the muscles in their arms, shoulders, and hands screamed for relief from carrying their precious load. The coarse brown cloth had served its purpose as a litter admirably well, but with only a handful of steps left to the tomb, it began to rip, so they stopped and eased the body to the ground.

"It's probably just as well," Nicodemus said, looking at the split in the cloth. "I can go no further,"

Not once as they trudged along had Joseph turned back to look at Nicodemus, but seeing his flushed face, he grew anxious. "Sit down, my friend. You must rest."

Nicodemus didn't argue. He managed to walk a couple of steps and collapsed onto a large boulder.

"While you rest I'll draw some water from the well so we can wash the body," Joseph said as he massaged his aching fingers. "I didn't have time to purchase oil and spices to prepare the body but at least we can get it washed."

"Look inside the tomb," Nicodemus said in an exhausted voice. "You will find all we need there."

Joseph looked at Nicodemus, perplexed, and was about to ask a question when Nicodemus continued. "Earlier this afternoon, just as the storm clouds gathered, I bought seventy-five pounds of oil, spices, and ointment and had it delivered to the tomb."

"But," Joseph asked, even more perplexed, "how did you know of the tomb?"

"A few days ago I went to Zophar, the stone hewer, to discuss a special gift I wanted him to create for Anna. I saw some beautiful stone he had piled in his shop and asked him about it. He told me about the tomb you had commissioned him to build." Nicodemus paused slightly and rubbed his aching neck. "Early this afternoon, when I told Anna of Jesus's crucifixion, it was she who figured out who the tomb was for. She also suggested I buy the oil and ointment."

Joseph walked over to Nicodemus and placed a hand on the man's shoulder. "Bless you, and bless Anna." And with sadness in his voice as he reflected on the relationship with his own wife, he softly added, "You are fortunate to have a wife so insightful and devoted as she."

Joseph walked the short distance to the small well and picked up the bucket lying beside the rocks that surrounded the well's deep shaft. Coiling the rope that was attached to the handle around his hand, he cautiously lowered the bucket into the darkness of the well and let the bucket fill with water. Drawing the full bucket, he detached the rope and took it with him to the entrance of the tomb.

The huge stone that would seal the tomb had been pushed even further from the opening, allowing easy access. Walking inside, Joseph again admired the beauty and craftsmanship. It truly was fit for a king, and the King of Kings would be its inhabitant. Neatly placed near the entrance were jars, pots, and rags. Joseph lifted the lid from two of the jars, and rich smells of aromatic spices filled his nostrils. Dipping a finger in one of the pots, he gently swirled the translucent oil and offered a silent prayer of thanks for the thoughtfulness of Nicodemus and Anna. He picked two rags from among a pile and took them and the bucket of water to where Nicodemus was sitting on a small rock beside the body of Jesus.

"Do you have enough energy to help me?" Joseph asked kindly.

"Of course! What would you like me to do?"

Joseph held out a rag and the water bucket. "Help me wash the body."

With the tenderness of a mother washing a newborn infant, the two men began their solemn task. Nicodemus poured a small stream of water from the bucket as Joseph gently lifted Jesus' head and rinsed mud and blood from his shoulder-length hair. Repeatedly soaking rags with water, each man then carefully wiped mud, dirt, grime, and blood from his arms, legs, and body until it was clean. Finally, only the wounds in his hands, feet, and side remained.

They worked in silence, each man anticipating the needs of the other. Delicately lifting Jesus's right hand, Joseph held it out while Nicodemus drizzled water into the mangled flesh of the palm. Particles of blood and dirt drained through the wound and dripped from the back of the hand, which Joseph wiped clean with a rag. Shifting to the other side of body, they did the same with his left hand and then moved to his feet. Finally, only the gash in the side of the body remained.

The ruthlessness with which the soldier had pierced his side was evident in the lacerated flesh. At different times, both men raced from the body's side and wretched what little contents were in their stomachs into the bushes in the garden.

With the washing complete, Joseph took the small bundle of beautiful white linen into the tomb and carefully spread it out on the rock ledge where they would lay Jesus's body. Returning to Nicodemus, who stood over the body, he said, "I think it will be best if we anoint his body with oil in the tomb rather than out here."

"I agree," said Nicodemus. "How shall we move the body?"

"I will do it myself," Joseph said, and in one graceful movement, he squatted beside the body and scooped it up in his arms. Walking to the tomb he carefully maneuvered his way through the entrance and laid the body on the linen cloth.

Nicodemus entered the tomb behind Joseph and walked to the jars of fragrant oil and ointments. Beside them was a small stack of undergarments, which he was grateful that Anna insisted he have delivered to the tomb along with the ointment. He picked them up and carried them to where Joseph stood. Handing them to Joseph, he then went back and picked up two jars of oil and ointment and returned to Joseph's side.

As gently as they could, the two men rubbed the oil and ointment over Jesus's bruised and battered body and the wounds in his hands, feet, and side. The oil's delicate aroma of roses and lilacs flooded their noses and filled the air. Finished with the oil, the men applied spices as they dressed the body in the undergarments and began the process of winding the clean white linen cloth tightly around the body.

Their task completed, the men carefully positioned the body, now wrapped completely in white, on the rock ledge and stepped back, studying their work. "Come, Joseph," Nicodemus said as he took the man by the elbow. "We must hurry. The Sabbath hour is fast approaching."

"I can't thank you enough for your help, Nicodemus. It would have been impossible for me to do this alone," he said, reluctantly backing away.

"You forget, Joseph, that he was also my Savior," Nicodemus said as he gathered pots and jars in his arms.

"I haven't forgotten, my friend." Joseph picked up the remaining pots and pile of rags. "This will not be easy for us," Joseph said, following Nicodemus from the tomb and setting down the pots and rags beside those Nicodemus had carried. "But we must now roll the stone over the entrance."

"Just the two of us?" Nicodemus exclaimed as he eyed the massive round stone.

"Yes," Joseph said. He stepped up and leaned his back against the cool stone. "I'll squat down and push against it with my back. If you can lean into the edge with your shoulder, I think the two of us, old and decrepit as we are, can roll it into place."

Doing as instructed, Nicodemus took his position. "On the count of three," Joseph said, "push for all you're worth. One, two, three!"

Whether it was a burst of adrenaline or the helping hand of God, the huge stone rolled down the slight decline and didn't stop until it lodged in its intended final resting place. "It is finished," Joseph exclaimed, wiping his hands on his robe. "And now you must go quickly, Nicodemus, so you can be home before the Sabbath begins."

"And what of you, Joseph?" Nicodemus asked without moving. "You too must be on your way home."

"Don't worry about me," Joseph said as he gave Nicodemus a gentle shove to encourage his departure. "I'll be fine."

Joseph stood in front of the tomb and watched as his friend hurried along the uneven path, taking him from the garden. As Nicodemus rounded a bend and disappeared from sight, Joseph drew his dirty cloak more tightly around him and lowered himself onto a small wooden and stone bench that someone had placed near the entrance of the tomb. Whether it was his physical exhaustion or a craftsman's good workmanship, Joseph found the bench was far more comfortable than he expected, and his body completely relaxed as he sat down. *Someone has placed this bench in the perfect location*, Joseph thought as he marveled at the golden sunset. Far in the distance, the sun was slipping down in the western sky, lengthening the shadows of the olive and Cypress trees in the garden. In not many minutes, he thought, it would sink below the hills, signaling the beginning of the Sabbath.

"The Sabbath, the seventh day, the end of the week," Joseph said softly to himself, "and the end of my life as I know it." His Savior was gone, placed in a tomb; his wife was gone, unwilling to allow him his beliefs; his position in the Sanhedrin would soon be gone, ended by Caiaphas's scheming; his business would fail, a casualty of his beliefs. And for all that was lost, something of far greater worth had been gained. Joseph let out a deep sigh, settled back into the comfort of the bench, and folded his hands across his chest. Closing his eyes, he slipped into sleep.

TWENTY

✻ ✻ ✻ ✻ ✻ ✻ ✻

The voice calling his name was sweet and gentle: "Joseph."
It was spoken so softly and tenderly it filled him with
peace and happiness. "Joseph," it came a second time, no louder
than the first, but more distinct and so delicate and loving.
Then he felt the soft stroke of fingers against his cheek, so slight
but so real. A gentle nudge to his forearm gradually pulled him
from sleep, and he slowly opened his eyes.

The sinking sun silhouetted the form in front of him,
and a soft glow seemed to radiate from the white robe. Joseph
blinked to clear his vision. A third time he heard his name, and
it was then that Joseph recognized the voice he had come to
know so well.

She stood motionless before him, her body inclined
slightly forward and her outstretched hand resting lightly on
his forearm. The remains of sleep instantly fled and he said,
"Devorah?"

She nodded her head but said nothing as she straightened
up and took a small step backward.

Joseph clamored to his feet, the muscles in his body rebel-
ling at having to move so quickly. "Why are you here?" Joseph
asked cautiously, unable to camouflage his surprise at seeing
her. "And how did you find me?"

"I've been searching for you for hours, ever since the storm stopped," she answered, lifting the scarf from off her head and draping it around her shoulders.

"But—" Joseph began, only to be cut off by Devorah.

"I looked everywhere I could imagine you might be. I'd given up and was going home when, by good fortune, I saw Nicodemus leaving the garden. He told me where to find you."

Joseph nodded his head in understanding, but cautiously asked, "But why? Why were you looking for me?"

Devorah swallowed and said with a smile, "Because I love you."

Joseph looked at her, unsure of what to do. His happiness at seeing her, combined with what she just said, made him want to take her in his arms and hug her, but that was dampened by his wariness over the things she had said during their last conversation. "I'm confused, Devorah," he finally managed to say.

Devorah took a deep breath and slowly exhaled. "I spent several hours this afternoon with Anna. She told me that she and Nicodemus believe in Jesus."

Joseph nodded but said nothing, waiting for her to continue.

Devorah shifted her feet and pulled her scarf more tightly around her neck to ward off the chill and dampness of the spring evening. "She explained many things to me, Joseph, some of which I find difficult to believe. But we talked of other things, things that spoke to my heart and filled me with peace and warmth."

Joseph looked at her, and a soft smile formed on his lips.

"I am not a believer in Jesus, at least not yet," Devorah said, "but I am a believer in you. I trust you, Joseph. I trust your judgment. And if I don't yet accept Him as my Savior and the Messiah, I believe in you and have faith in your beliefs. And for the present time, that is enough for me."

A flood of love, appreciation, and gratitude swept over

Joseph as he stood looking into his wife's deep brown eyes. Without saying a word, he stepped close to her and encircled her in his arms, pulling her close to him. Devorah rested her head against his chest, wrapped her arms tightly around his waist, and they stood solidly together.

They held each other in silence for several minutes, watching the last rays of the setting sun disappear. Without looking at her, Joseph said, "You realize there will be difficult days ahead. Life for us will be different than it has been in the past. Are you certain you can accept that?"

Tilting her head up to face him, she said, "I would rather go through difficult days with you than have an easy life without you."

Joseph smiled, inclined his head downward and kissed her.

EPILOGUE

Joseph woke with a start and sat up, looking anxiously around the room. Relief swept over him when, even in the semi-darkness of the early morning, he saw all the familiar surroundings of his bedroom and realized the desert, camels, heat, and sand had all been a dream. But it was so vivid and real, unlike any dream he'd ever had before. He could feel the grit of the sand in his teeth and smell the foul breath of the camel as he led it to the watering hole. And the details of the explicit conversation with the stranger—no, *messenger*—were indelibly etched in his mind as was every twist and turn in the trail they were following. No, this was no ordinary dream. This was a vision!

Joseph lay back on the pillow, thinking about what he had just experienced. *Dreams fade quickly*, he told himself, *and this isn't fading*. It was all there in amazing detail with instant recall.

Joseph rolled over and lightly shook Devorah by the shoulder. "Devorah, wake up. I need to tell you something."

Devorah groaned but only pulled the covers up more tightly over her head.

"Devorah," Joseph said more loudly and gave her a more forceful shake. "Wake up!"

"What is it?" she said as she rolled over to face him, her

head still buried under the covers.

"You must wake up, Devorah. This is important."

Groggily, Devorah tossed the covers from off her head and slowly propped herself on one elbow. "I'm awake," she said, still far more asleep than awake. "What is it?"

For more than an hour, he told Devorah the details of his vision. He began with a description of the messenger who outlined future events that would befall Jerusalem. He explained the instructions the messenger had given him on disposing of his property and business and the things he was to purchase with the money. Joseph went on in great detail about a journey they were to take and how the messenger said they would be led in their travels to a choice land. He explained the instructions the messenger gave him about the others he was to tell about the pending journey.

Several times as Joseph spoke, he looked at Devorah and wondered how she was receiving everything he was saying. It had only been seven days since he had placed Jesus in the tomb and although she was trying mightily, he could tell she struggled with misgivings. In that week, Joseph had taken Devorah to an upper room in a small house where they met with a group of Jesus's followers. Peter had been there and taught Jesus's doctrine, but Devorah confided in Joseph afterward that it had been Mary, the mother of Jesus, who had given her the greatest insight.

Devorah patiently listened to Joseph. Only twice during his retelling of the vision did she stop him—once to ask a question about how quickly they were to proceed and once to get more details about the instructions the messenger had given about their children and grandchildren. When Joseph concluded his description of the vision, he looked at her with an unspoken question in his eyes, which Devorah answered by reaching up and patting him lightly on the cheek. "I believed in you a week ago, and I believe in you still. We'll move forward together."

Thirty days later, Caiaphas plumped down in the chair next to Simeon and tried his best not to let a huge grin spread over his face, and for the most part, he succeeded. "This has turned out better than I could have imagined," he whispered.

Trying to maintain some semblance of decorum, Simeon suppressed his own smile and spoke out of the corner of his mouth. "Much, much better."

The discussion lasted only a few minutes, much less than Caiaphas had expected, and there had been virtually no debate. With only forty-eight of the Sanhedrin's members present in the chamber, Caiaphas stood up and announced the first matter for their consideration was Joseph of Arimathea, or more exactly, the expulsion of Joseph of Arimathea from the Sanhedrin. A chorus of whispers spread through the room as if this was the first any of them had heard of it, when in fact the only question in the minds of most of those present was why it had taken Caiaphas so long to bring the matter for a formal vote.

No one in the room doubted for a minute that Joseph would be removed. There could be no forgiveness for his actions. Given enough time and penance on Joseph's part, they probably could have excused his daring speech on the floor of the Sanhedrin when he proclaimed that Jesus was the Messiah, but they simply couldn't overlook his participation in the removal and burial of Jesus's body. And as if to add salt to the wound, he had placed Christ's body in his own tomb, no less! It was too shocking and too blatant to overlook. There was no choice—he had to be removed.

A slightly more thorny issue was Nicodemus, and that was the reason it had taken so long to bring the matter of Joseph to a vote. Caiaphas had hoped to remove the two men at the same time, in one grand action, but on the issue of Nicodemus, there was considerable disagreement. Caiaphas had pushed hard but was never able to persuade or coerce enough members into even considering his expulsion. His defenders had asked what the man had done that had been so egregious to warrant removal. He had not publicly proclaimed Jesus to be the Messiah as Joseph had done. And it was only hearsay that he had assisted in the removal and burial of the body. No, Nicodemus was quite secure in his position, even if he hadn't attended a single session since Jesus had been crucified.

"You learned men have heard the charges against Joseph of Arimathea," Caiaphas boomed after he had carefully outlined them in great detail. "What say you, brethren? Do we expel the man?" A loud and thunderous shout of yes echoed off the walls, and it was over—Joseph of Arimathea was no longer a member of the Sanhedrin.

Caiaphas replaced the smirk on his face with a more austere look befitting his role as chief high priest as he stood there. In spite of the satisfaction the decision gave him and his wish to relish the moment, he reluctantly introduced another matter that must be considered—a discussion about how many steps a man could walk without breaking the Sabbath.

With the discussion underway, Caiaphas returned to his seat beside Simeon and couldn't resist the opportunity to gloat. "I expected discussion or disagreement, at least someone to stand in his defense and drag the discussion on for an hour or more, but it was finished in only a few minutes."

Simeon nodded his head slightly to acknowledge he heard the comment, but offered no response. He too wanted members of the Sanhedrin to think he was earnestly listening to Barnabas, an ancient old Pharisee, as he defended walking one thousand steps on the Sabbath.

Likewise, Caiaphas pretended to pay attention, but his mind was far away. In truth, Caiaphas had to admit to himself that while his lobbying efforts had assured Joseph's removal, of far more significance was Joseph's expulsion from the synagogue the week before. By being excommunicated from the synagogue, Joseph no longer had standing in the Jewish community. He was an outcast, a stranger in his own town. He would be avoided, ignored, and ridiculed by other Jews, no longer one of the chosen children of Israel, but a heathen. Once excommunicated from the synagogue, there was simply no way he could function in the Sanhedrin, so his expulsion was really a foregone conclusion.

Caiaphas would have reveled in the moment even more except for one issue: Devorah. As happy as he was about Joseph's fall from power and position, he had a twinge of sorrow for his cousin, for she would feel some of the effects as well. The wealthy Greeks and other Gentiles in the community wouldn't care whether Joseph was excommunicated or not, but the Jews would distance themselves from her, and over time, they would avoid her altogether. If she could bring herself to attend the synagogue on the Sabbath, which she probably wouldn't do, she would be politely, and not so politely, ignored. And then there would be the gossip. Behind her back she would be the subject of countless wagging tongues.

Caiaphas had placed all these issue in the balance when weighing what role to play in Joseph's excommunication. He had to go from the Sanhedrin, there was no debate about that, but the issue of his excommunication from the synagogue was a slightly different matter. For a brief time, he had considered pushing for Joseph's censure, not his excommunication, but that had occurred in a moment of weakness out of concern for Devorah. In the end, he decided the loss of her friendship was a small price to pay for humiliating her husband, so he pushed for his excommunication from the synagogue. He'd had the briefest moment of guilt over his decision, but it had fled when he reminded himself he had given her a chance to side with him, and she had opted for her husband instead. She made her choice—now she would have to live with it.

Simeon's voice jolted Caiaphas back to the present. Resting his elbow on the arm of his chair and inclining his body toward Caiaphas, he whispered out of the corner of his mouth, "I'm told Joseph is selling out his business."

"Really?" Caiaphas asked, genuinely surprised.

"So it would seem. And for far less than its value too," Simeon said.

"But why?" Caiaphas asked. "Certainly he could turn it over to his sons."

"That's another strange thing," Simeon said, turning to look directly at Caiaphas, not really caring who might be watching their conversation at this point. "All four of his sons have sold their houses, flocks, and vineyards."

At this, Caiaphas turned completely in his chair and faced Simeon. "When did this happen?"

"I'm not certain. From what I'm told, they have been going about it quietly, so as not to attract any attention.

"Puzzling," was all Caiaphas said and leaned back in his chair, churning over in his mind this latest bit of news while feigning attention to Barnabas and his droning.

While the Sanhedrin debated Joseph's fate, Joseph, Devorah, their four sons, and each of their wives, and all their grandchildren assembled in Joseph's home in the upper city. While children and grandchildren excitedly talked in the courtyard about the adventure that awaited them, Joseph and Devorah walked hand in hand through each room in the sprawling mansion. It was no longer their home. As part of the transaction in which Joseph sold his business to Constantine, the rotund Greek merchant with whom he had done business for years, he also offered to sell the sprawling and impressive home for a very reasonable price. The short, talkative Greek could hardly believe his good fortune at the opportunity and jumped at the chance.

The rooms were empty of furniture, and the walls were bare of art work, all of it sold to neighbors at drastically reduced prices. The couple made their way to the veranda for one last view of the city. The trees were in full leaf, and the smell of blossoms filled the air. This was Joseph's favorite place in his home. From here he had a sweeping view of Jerusalem. Letting go of Devorah's hand, he walked to the railing and peered between tall cypress trees to a hill in the distance. There, in the garden, just below the crown of the hill, he could make out the round stone that guarded the tomb's entrance. Joseph stood silently for several minutes as a sense of gratitude and peace filled his heart. The tomb was empty, and for that Joseph rejoiced.

"Come, Joseph, it's time for us to leave," Devorah said, walking up beside her husband and intertwining her fingers in his.

Joseph smiled at his wife and squeezed her hand. "Yes," he said softly, "it is time." They turned from the veranda and walked to the courtyard to join the rest of the family.

"Let's be on our way," Joseph said, and he pushed open the gate and led the group onto the street.

The younger grandchildren jumped, skipped, and raced ahead of Joseph and Devorah as they walked down the broad avenue in the morning sunlight. Older grandchildren joked and laughed and immediately needed constant prodding from their parents to keep up with the others. As the small group neared Nicodemus's house, Joseph could see his aged friend and his wife along with their children and grandchildren already waiting outside the gate to their home. With joyous salutations, the two groups joined into one and continued down the street.

Passing Caiaphas's estate, Joseph turned to Devorah and said, "He thinks he's destroyed me and destroyed Jesus, but this is only the beginning."

Devorah smiled and said, "Yes, the beginning for us and the beginning of the end for him."

The little group had only gone as far as the city gates when four-year-old Chasid tugged on his grandfather's flowing cloak. "Poppa, my legs are tired. Will you carry me on your shoulders?"

Smiling, Joseph bent over, scooped the little boy in his arms, and hoisted him up in the air. "Of course I will, but be sure and tell me the moment you see the pens and shelters," Joseph said.

"I will, Poppa. I promise," he said, clasping his hands under Joseph's chin.

An hour later, the small group turned off the main road leading from Jerusalem and wound their way along an almost indistinguishable stony trail. Working through brush and scrubby trees, they crested a small hill, and young Chasid, still on Joseph's shoulders, said, "I see them, Poppa. I see them!" And see them he did. In a small valley below them were several pens filled with camels, donkeys, sheep, and goats. Several men scurried around the pens, tossing in armfuls of fodder and carrying buckets of water from the spring that flowed nearby. Beyond the pens, several women were busy cooking food over a small fire and arranging assorted items under crudely constructed shelters.

"Who are those people?" Chasid asked.

"Servants from our home in Jerusalem," Joseph said. "They have decided to join us in our journey."

"What's all that over there?" Chasid asked, pointing to a small mountain of items stacked beneath crude shelters.

"Those are our tents, food, and other supplies we'll need for the next several months," Joseph replied as he lifted Chasid from his shoulders.

"This is going to be fun!" Chasid called over his shoulder as he raced down the trail toward the pens.

Joseph looked at his wife who was walking beside him.

"I'm not certain how much fun it will be, but I'm certain it's the right thing to do."

At sunrise the following morning, the group began their trek. And though it was unknown to Joseph or any of his fellow travelers, they were following the same route that had been used six hundred years earlier, when another man and his family had been led by the hand of God from Jerusalem to a choice land.

ABOUT THE AUTHOR

E. James Harrison was born in Salt Lake City and developed an early love for and fascination with the great men and women of the Bible while sitting on his parents' couch flipping through the pages of *Bible Stories for Children*.

An avid student of the scriptures, he's been teaching (some might say confusing) youth and adults as a Sunday School teacher for over twenty years and is apparently destined to continue doing so until he gets it right or dies, whichever comes first.

A professional marketing communications consultant, he holds a bachelors degree with emphasis in creative writing and has written countless articles, newsletters, advertisements, and commercials. He has authored dozens of books in his mind, but this is the first he has committed to paper.

When not putting words on paper for himself or others, Jim can be found flying airplanes or boating with his family.

He and his wife Deborah live in St. George, Utah, and are the parents of two daughters.